PITCHED INTO LOVE

Steph Baxter's invitation to her friend's Scottish castle hotel results in her having to pitch in and help out during an emergency. She's assisted by the gorgeous half-owner Jack McGregor and soon, despite business worries and his father's health, his powerful feelings for Steph take priority. But with secrets in her past, trust isn't something she can readily give. Then, as Jack's brother and wife make a reappearance, old wounds challenge everything. Can new love survive the highland storms?

JUDY JARVIE

PITCHED INTO LOVE

Complete and Unabridged

LINFORD
Leicester

First published in Great Britain in 2012

First Linford Edition
published 2012

British Library CIP Data

Jarvie, Judy.
   Pitched into love. - -
   (Linford romance library)
   1. Love stories.
   2. Large type books.
   I. Title II. Series
   823.9'2–dc23

   ISBN 978–1–4448–1360–9

Published by
F. A. Thorpe (Publishing)
Anstey, Leicestershire

Set by Words & Graphics Ltd.
Anstey, Leicestershire
Printed and bound in Great Britain by
T. J. International Ltd., Padstow, Cornwall

This book is printed on acid-free paper

1

The rich voice came from out of the blue. 'Need some help? Bad timing for a flat tyre.'

Steph Baxter looked over her shoulder at the sleek, silver sports car then glanced at her jacked-up wheel.

'Looks like a downpour's coming. I could help if you like,' said the stranger through the small gap of lowered car window. He had dark hair and eyes — not that it particularly mattered, as right now he could be her only ray of hope.

'Sorry to trouble you,' Steph called back. 'But I can't get the wheel off, and without muscles like a weight lifter I'm never going to get it changed.'

A remote Highland road may offer great scenery but it wasn't ideal for a breakdown. So if help was on offer, why refuse?

'Hold on, I'll be with you in a second,' the man said, and in moments he'd parked up on the verge.

When he approached, Steph had her biggest shock; the tall stranger sported an expensive, formal dinner suit — black jacket, snow-white shirt and silk bow tie. He was what Steph imagined an international playboy would look like, but he pulled on a sensible wax jacket as he reached her.

'I didn't pump my muscles up this morning but I'll give it my best shot.' His grin was a killer; handsome yet boyish, with a hint of mischief thrown in.

Steph gave him a wan smile, embarrassed now by her talk of muscles. Sometimes her mouth went into overdrive before her brain chastised it and regulated the flow of chatter.

All she wanted was to get back on the road to Abercarrick, to reach her destination and to chill out over dinner with her best friend, Ally. She was on her way to stay at her friends' castle hotel, where interior designer Ally and chef Fraser were living the dream — this had been her first chance to visit.

'Right. Let's get you sorted.'

Steph looked at the stranger dubiously as she pushed back her dark blonde hair. He looked as if he'd just walked out of some designer store in Milan. 'Are you sure ... ? You're dressed for the Oscars. You might get dirty.'

The stranger chuckled. 'I'll keep my cuffs clean if it makes you feel better. We can't have you languishing here for want of a man with muscles.'

'You aren't going to let me forget that comment, are you?' Steph moved aside; she imagined the stranger probably thought she was a ninny woman driver. 'My brother's a mechanic. He showed me how to change a wheel but I didn't realise it was quite so strenuous.'

'Sometimes the bolts can be tough to budge.' The stranger's teeth were white against bronzed skin. In a matter of seconds he'd loosened the bolts. 'There. With luck we'll have you sorted before the weather turns. They've been warning of rain today and it could be a bad one. Muggy air, threat of thunder.'

'You spoke too soon.' Steph pulled her hood up as the rain suddenly started in earnest. The smell of a summer downpour on hot earth and Tarmac was one she'd always relished — but this was a hard-core flood.

The stranger rose. 'We should take cover. My car or yours?'

Was getting into a car with a strange man wise? Or was getting soaked out of caution plain silly? Some would probably advise steadfast resistance, but it felt like foolishness to start getting antsy when this passer-by was helping her out.

He must have sensed her hesitancy because he shrugged then handed his keys over. 'Take these and sit in my car. You're right to be wary; I'll stay and tough it out.'

Steph bit her lip. Her jeans were

soaked from the knees down and water cascaded from her hood. 'My conscience couldn't stand it if you drowned. C'mon.'

They ran at speed to his sports car. Once in the passenger seat, Steph pulled at her soggy clothes. 'I feel terrible. You're in your best gear and you're soaked through. You should've driven on by.'

The stranger shrugged as he wiped his face. 'I've borne worse and I'm coming back from a dinner anyway.' His voice was deep and the accent was Scottish. His eyes glittered, causing her a surprising inner tremble of awareness. 'You don't sound local,' he added.

Steph knew her friend, Ally, would agree this man was gorgeous. She schooled herself not to notice. *You're off men, remember,* she told herself. *You're working out your future, and forgetting the past.*

'I'm from London, heading to the Highlands to stay with friends. I stayed in the Lake District last night.' Steph

5

nodded to the relentless rain beating down on the windscreen. 'It was beautiful an hour ago. The mountains bathed in sun were stunning — and I have photos to prove it.'

Steph realised most women would be batting their eyelashes; instead she was boring him with her small-talk. 'D'you think it'll stop soon?' she asked.

'It'll ease when it's ready,' he said. 'Four seasons in one day; that's Scotland. But actually, that's what makes it so lush and green. It's rugged and harsh at times but gloriously beautiful at its best.'

'You should do tourist ads,' Steph replied. 'I'm in marketing and that was a cracking off-the-cuff promotion. If I still had a job I'd employ you.'

'*Had* a job?'

Steph wished she hadn't gone there; now she'd have to explain. 'I was made redundant, without warning — ten years' work down the drain.'

It was part of the reason she'd come here; to work out a life plan, to reconsider and replenish her reserves. To work out what she really wanted to do with her life and forget the disappointments that had jaded her in so many ways.

'I'm sorry to hear that.' He held out a hand. 'I'm Jack, by the way.' His grip was strong and the contact made her skin tingle.

'I'm Steph,' she replied. 'And thanks again for helping.'

'Of course,' Jack added wryly, 'you realise I'll have to get that tyre off. My muscles couldn't stand the inferiority complex.'

'I won't judge. I'm causing puddles on the floor of your car.'

'It looks like it's clearing. Shall we risk it?' Jack quirked an eyebrow in challenge.

'I'm game if you are.'

As they got back to their mission, Steph's mobile phone rang in her pocket.

'Ally's in hospital.' Fraser, Ally's husband, sounded in a state of near panic. 'She fainted earlier on and the ambulance took her. I'm with her now.'

Steph felt her pulse race as she fought shock reflexes. Ally was seven-and-a-half months pregnant.

'She's been feeling dizzy and they want to keep an eye on her, so I won't be there when you arrive at the hotel, I'm afraid. I'll explain later when we meet.'

'Are she and the baby okay?' Steph asked.

'They're stable. Ally just needs rest.'

'Give her my love.' Steph rubbed her temple at the shock news. An extra pair of hands had just become essential at the Glen Muir Hotel, Abercarrick.

Jack had changed the wheel and was tightening bolts like a seasoned pro. The rain hadn't put him off his stride — he was the kind of man who clearly rose to any crisis. 'Bad news?'

'My friend's in hospital.'

'Sorry to hear that.' Jack looked up at her with honest, serious blue eyes. 'Well, that's you done,' he said, stowing the tools away.

'Thanks,' she said, 'I really appreciate it.'

'Safe journey. I hope your friend's okay.'

Her roadside saviour strolled back to his car, as if playing the hero was just part of the day job. And, going by first impressions, Steph guessed it probably was.

★　★　★

Steph sat in the hotel's main reception, a crackling log fire her only company. Her eyelids drooped but she wouldn't head for bed without hearing news of Ally first.

When she finally arrived in Abercarrick, her optimism of the last few days had collapsed. One row of cottages, a postbox and church completed the landscape. The high-towered Glen Muir Castle Hotel sat on the edge of the loch like something straight from a history book.

Steph plumped a cushion, then

curled back on the sofa beneath her jacket. This wasn't how she'd imagined her first night here, but all she wanted was an all-clear on Ally.

'Camping out?'

A male voice broke her solitude but she smiled when she saw the voice's owner. 'Jack.'

'Small world. I can't believe we're meeting again — what brings you here?' His dark brows had risen in surprise and it was suddenly so good to see a face she recognised. 'It seems destiny is throwing us together — either that, or you're having a terrible run of luck. Did you decide to break your journey? Or is it more car problems?'

His tuxedo was gone and he stood tall and muscular in faded jeans and a rugby shirt, arms crossed across an impressive broad chest. His smile was as dazzling as she remembered, and he approached her in easy strides.

She grinned back, feeling like a schoolgirl meeting a favourite pal. 'This is where I'm staying, actually. Don't tell me you've broken down, too?'

Steph felt her pulse quicken. He was ruggedly appealing and his profile alone would have inspired any sculptor. What was it about this guy that made her react?

'I work here, actually. The name's Jack McGregor.'

'Steph Baxter. You must know Ally and Fraser if you work here then? They're owners of Glen Muir. Have you heard any news?'

'Fraser's just called to tell me he's staying at the hospital; Ally's sleeping and he's been persuaded not to risk driving while he's so tired. Have you checked in yet?' Jack looked at the empty reception desk behind them, then walked over to it.

She motioned to her bags. 'No. I'll book in now that I know Ally's all right, though.'

'Why don't I have your bags taken up? Then you can come to the bar for a drink if you like. I suspect you deserve one.'

11

Steph rose from her seat, feeling her aching muscles protest. She felt exhausted, but a nightcap was probably the best remedy. 'Sounds great, but I don't want to monopolise your time, especially not if you're working.'

'I'm always working, but welcoming guests is part of the deal.' Jack's gaze met hers with a burning intensity. He stopped as if trying to find the right words and cleared his throat before proceeding. 'There's something you should know; Fraser and Ally are actually my business partners. I'm part owner here at Glen Muir. Coming to the bar, then?'

'If you twist my arm hard enough . . .' Steph pushed her hair from her face with one hand, accidentally catching her bracelet in the strands as she did so.

In two strides Jack was beside her. 'Here, let me.' He took her wrist and gently loosened the bracelet catch to free her tangled hair. The light pressure of his skin caused tingles to run up her arm and she shivered, despite the fire beside them.

Was she just tired and imagining chemistry here?

'There, you're free,' he told her softly.

She might be free of the bracelet, but the palpitations and butterflies had taken full hold. This man affected her and made it hard to breathe normally, especially when his eyes had more heat in their glittering depths than the open log fire beside them. Steph stared back into his intense, blue gaze as the semi-smile on his lips caused her skin to prickle.

Suddenly, a door to the right clicked open and they both looked up to see a beautiful blonde woman watching them with interested pale, blue eyes.

'I wondered where you'd got to. Not interrupting anything, am I?' Her tone had an accusatory edge and Steph wondered who she was.

Steph blushed as Jack dropped her wrist. Their discussion by the fireside had been innocent enough, but the proximity of it looked incriminating.

But if Jack McGregor had a girlfriend

or partner, why was he inviting her for drinks?

'Hilary . . . apologies, I got side-tracked.' Jack's jaw tightened.

'Who's your friend?' asked Hilary coolly.

'Steph Baxter, a friend of Ally and Fraser's.'

Steph forced a smile as she said, 'Nice to meet you, Hilary. I'll skip the bar invitation and check in now, Jack. I'm more tired than I realised.'

Hilary wrapped herself around his arm. The woman was polished and attractive, but there was something very feline and a touch predatory about her too.

'Do I have to keep sending out a search-party for you, darling? You're the Laird of Glen Muir; you mustn't keep getting distracted by petty details.'

Feeling as if she'd just been dismissed as a 'petty detail' herself, Steph picked up her bags.

'I'll get someone to escort you,' Jack said firmly and rang the reception bell

14

somewhat brusquely. Steph noticed that colour spotted his cheeks. 'Shall we go, Hilary?'

The desk clerk emerged as they left but Steph still prickled with awkwardness. The Laird of Glen Muir may be charming, but she told herself she should keep him at arms' length.

'Staying long?' asked the concierge conversationally.

After today's twists and mishaps, Steph realised she couldn't be sure.

'Undecided as yet,' she answered truthfully, and trudged off to find her room.

2

Steph's first night was plagued by her recurring dream. She was back in Rhodes, chasing Charlie who was on the scooter. She was running and shouting — 'Don't be crazy, Charlie!' — but to no avail . . .

Panting and sweating, she sat bolt upright in bed after she woke; her heartbeat drumming, her chest tight with fatigue, throat hoarse from crying out and the clammy veil of hot sweat soaking through her nightclothes.

It was just as it had been four years ago on the island . . . the villa, the potent scent of the rosemary bushes in the garden . . . the scooter . . .

In her dreams she was fighting to make him listen.

Four years ago she'd given up trying to make him see sense. She'd told him she couldn't take it any more and he'd driven away in a cloud of hot dust and fury — without a helmet or much knowledge of scooter riding and on winding, unfamiliar Greek island roads.

But Charlie had always thought he knew better. Wasn't that just where he'd always gone wrong?

Steph lay in the darkness, trying to calm her breathing. She may have reached Scotland but she couldn't escape her past.

* * *

Next morning, Steph went to breakfast determined to keep any contact with Jack McGregor low-key. She was only here to see and support Ally and Fraser Munro and she didn't need entanglements — or feuds with local women — marring her stay. If necessary, she'd tell Jack plainly.

She entered a majestic panelled dining room that boasted awe-inspiring mountain views across the loch. She was quickly guided to a table by a smiling waiter and had just started to scan the menu when she saw Fraser approaching.

'Fraser, you're back!'

And thank goodness he was, she thought; she needed to know about Ally. Fraser's strain was evident; his face was drawn and his eyes looked tired. She slid a hand around his shoulders to give him a reassuring hug. 'Is she okay?'

'She's stable but they're keeping her under observation. I'll go back later . . . they said she has a low placenta and they want to ensure rest is her priority, for the safety of the baby.'

Steph squeezed Fraser's arm. 'She's in the best place. Worrying yourself silly won't help.' Steph plastered on her best encouraging smile. 'We all have to stay positive and give Ally all the peace and space she needs.'

Fraser squeezed Steph's hand in return. 'Your being here will cheer Ally no end — and you always did manage to stop me from wallowing.' He gave her a wan smile.

'Actually, I feel like I'm dreaming — this castle's fantastic but it's all a bit surreal, too.'

'It's some place, isn't it? When things calm down a bit I'll make sure you get the grand tour. Feel free to look around and explore.'

Steph saw Jack approaching through the arched dining room entranceway. He looked sharp but casual in granite chinos and a pale grey sweater. She cast her glance away, unsure of how to react after the night before.

'Knowing Ally is out of danger makes it worth the journey,' she said to Fraser. 'What happened?'

Fraser sighed. 'Doing too much — you know Ally, she never stops. She'd climbed a ladder to clean windows and then felt dizzy and fainted. She needs to save her energies.'

'Fraser,' Jack said, stopping beside their table. 'My apologies for interrupting. I've scheduled in extra kitchen cover, so you can just relax and take good care of your wife. Spend as much time at the hospital as you both need.'

When Fraser explained about Ally's present condition, Jack answered, 'At the risk of sounding like the boring doctor, pregnancy takes a lot out of a woman's body. Sometimes nature steps in to make you take things slower. I'm sure the rest will do both mother and baby good.'

Steph stared at Jack in open surprise. Had he really just said he was a doctor? The waiter came with coffee, and Steph ordered her breakfast and encouraged Fraser to join her. Jack swiftly excused himself and told Fraser he'd be in his office if he was needed.

'He's a doctor as well as your partner?' she asked Fraser when Jack disappeared.

'GP at the local medical centre. He only got involved in the running of the estate after his brother left halfway through our restoration of the castle. He's a great business partner.'

'Is there anything Jack McGregor doesn't do?' Steph laughed somewhat nervously. 'He runs a hotel, he's a laird, a doctor, he restored a castle — he even fixed my tyre by the roadside yesterday. He gets around. Mr Fix it.'

'He's loyal, trustworthy and decent,' Fraser responded earnestly. 'I trust Jack like a brother.'

Steph took a breath to speak, but chose not to raise the subject of Jack's private life and the mysterious Hilary.

Fraser changed tack and went on. 'I'd appreciate if you could help around the hotel, Steph. Jess our housekeeper will stand in and show you the ropes, but an extra pair or hands and eyes would be invaluable. We've a few busy weeks ahead.'

'I'll try but . . . ' Steph began but then Fraser stopped her, his face a picture of shock.

'I've just remembered! There's meant to be a Highland fair here on Saturday — crafts, cookery demonstrations, a band, dancers, Reiki and aromatherapy treatments, the works! It's a big local attraction and usually well attended. It was Ally's brainchild and she usually handles it, but . . . oh, could you speak to Jack about it for me . . . please?'

'Fraser, I'm a novice,' Steph warned.

'You ran a big marketing department in London. You used to organise fairs at Olympia and Earl's Court. Jack and Jess will help, but I'm sure it'll almost run itself.'

Perhaps it wasn't the fair that bothered her so much as the handsome laird's presence? Steph stuffed her misgivings deep because Fraser had enough worries without her dithering.

'I'll try my best.' She put her coffee cup to her lips. 'How hard can it be?'

'Wishing you hadn't come yet?' Fraser added apologetically.

'Well, you certainly know how to test a girl before she's even had her breakfast,' Steph returned, laughing.

⋆ ⋆ ⋆

Jack McGregor took a drink of too-strong, lukewarm Columbian coffee and flicked through Hilary's lacklustre but expensive report. If this was what management consultants did, he decided he'd be better off without one.

Jack may be proficient in diagnosing medical problems but it didn't follow that he could solve business ailments as readily. Sadly there was no easy remedy for recession, bank stringency and hard business times. Glen Muir Hotel needed more money and the bank wanted a marketing plan to support extra financial backing. He'd hired Hilary to help. Big mistake.

She'd charged by the hour, her report was poor at best, and she'd spent three weeks in his hotel free to compile it; spa treatments, champagne and all the trimmings. Her 'Jack, darling' endearments and chasing him around had been further flies in an already sticky ointment with Hilary Benson.

Jack sighed, thinking of the other deadline fast closing in. The muscles in his jaw tensed as he punched in the number which he now knew by heart.

'It's Jack McGregor. Hello, Mrs Blaketon. How is my father this morning?'

'Hello, Dr McGregor. He's much more lucid today, but we have to be prepared for such episodes to become more frequent,' Mrs Blaketon answered. 'It's the way with dementia, as we both know.'

'Thanks for all your help with my father, and for alerting me to come straight away yesterday. It's best for me to be there.'

'I'm so sorry I disturbed your gala dinner.'

'No matter. My father is my first priority and I was pleased to leave the business association AGM anyhow. I'll drop by and see Dad later today — is that okay?'

'We'll see you then.'

Jack closed his eyes; the incident had shocked him and he'd had little sleep as a result. Even GPs had a tough time when facing family health problems. He'd still been in shock when he'd run into Steph by the roadside; but doing something useful had been a welcome escape from dwelling on things.

Dad needs professional care and he's in the best place, Jack told himself. So why did his plight still challenge him?

A vision of Steph's expression this morning ran through his head. He could tell he'd offended her in some way. Her dusty blonde hair and grey, searching eyes were etched in his mind, the way she'd looked at him today with wariness and mistrust.

He guessed that he should probably explain about Hilary. But why would Steph Baxter even care, and why did he feel compelled to point out that he and Hilary weren't an item?

Jack switched off the computer; he'd take a run by the loch, then he'd handle Hilary. Pounding his muscles would help fortify him for the task.

★ ★ ★

After breakfast, Steph took a leisurely mini-tour around the castle, which more than lived up to her expectations, followed by a stroll around the grounds, finishing up at the car park.

Unknowingly she'd timed it perfectly to see Hilary cross over to her car. She was loading a large pile of luggage into the boot of her scarlet sports car, her expression worse than before; riled stormy thunder with a grudge.

Jack stood nearby with his arms crossed, wearing sports gear. The pair shared brief terse words before Hilary slammed the car door sullenly with some words Steph didn't catch. She felt compelled to go over, and dashed towards Hilary's car, but it was already off up the gravel avenue at speed.

'Jack,' she said breathlessly.

'Good morning. You okay?' Jack's smile was genuine. Yet clearly a dispute had just taken place.

'If I've offended your girlfriend then I'm sorry. Last night felt like a case of two's company, with me most definitely the one causing the crowd.'

'Hilary isn't my girlfriend,' Jack replied in surprise. 'This has nothing to do with you. She was working on a hotel project and I didn't sanction her ideas. Or her conduct. And yes, you did pick up certain vibes last night — but it's nothing for you to feel bad about, truly.'

Relief coursed through Steph. She'd felt as if she'd inherited a grievance that wouldn't be resolved easily.

'Doesn't look as if she'll be back in a hurry.'

'Maybe that's because I insisted she pay some of her bill. It's been a long time coming, believe me.'

Steph blushed. Suddenly she felt intrusive and foolish. But last night she'd assumed Hilary and Jack had been an item.

'I thought you were a couple.'

'So did Hilary; without my consent. I'm happy staying single. At least, I am when it's Hilary who's chasing.' Jack gave her a wry look. A band of colour stained his cheekbones and Steph thought that he looked like a modesty-struck little boy.

Steph was suddenly aware she was blushing too. 'I'd best go. I'm meeting Jess, the housekeeper; apparently I'm helping to run a Highland fair. There's a first time for everything.'

Jack reached out and put a stalling hand on her arm. 'Then we should meet up later to discuss it. I'll be back from surgery early evening. Want to meet in the bar? Fraser mentioned you may need pointers and it's not fair to leave you in the lurch.'

'Seven would suit. I've already booked dinner here at eight.'

He shrugged. 'Seven it is, then. It'll make up for Hilary's rudeness last night.'

He smiled in a way that made her certain that the nurses and female patients at his medical centre must swoon whenever they witnessed it. Jack McGregor was the dashing doctor personified. And Steph knew that, try as she might, she wasn't immune. Was an antidote of good sense needed here?

'Got to dash. See you at seven.' His

smile still had her tummy turning somersaults as she watched him jog away, and she wondered why she'd just let herself admire those strong shoulders.

Maybe it was learning the truth about Hilary the Horrible. And that the dishy doctor was, in fact, single.

3

Steph met the vivacious, dark-haired housekeeper of Glen Muir, Jess Cameron, a short time later. She knew within minutes that they'd be firm friends thanks to Jess's easy manner, irreverent humour and infectious enthusiasm for life.

'I've heard so much about you and I've been longing for you to get here,' Jess said, her curls bouncing, after she took a booking on her phone system headset with calm ease. 'Ally says you're her confidante and I'd love you to bits.'

'Then Ally's over-hyped me. I'm redundant, at a loose end and I've even lost my flat because the landlord wants to sell up. I came here for some breathing space and thinking time.'

Jess empathised. 'It always all happens at once, eh?'

'You could say that. At work the axe-men called us out of the office one by one and told us to clear our desks. Overnight I was out of work.'

'But you'll soon get your fighting spirit back. You'll find a new job before long. What about a boyfriend? Won't he miss you while you're gone?'

Steph smoothed her trousers over her slim knees, then shrugged. 'I don't have a boyfriend. Once burned, and all that. I'm fine as I am.'

'Ah yes, fires burn, but remember, they're warm and comforting too, Steph. Sometimes an unexpected spark is just what's needed.'

Sensing Jess might just be Glen Muir's local matchmaker, Steph quickly changed topic. 'I understand you're going to give me a crash course in running a hotel?'

They quickly got down to the tasks in hand as Jess gave Steph a potted run-down of key duties and procedures. She covered the main day-to-day queries she could expect. It seemed manageable and there would be friendly staff at hand for help.

'Do you think I'll manage to have the Highland fair under control by Saturday?'

'Sure. Jack will give you the files. It's popular, so all the tickets are sold already; only last-minute details need checking. Have you settled into your room? Is everything satisfactory?'

'Couldn't ask for better.' Steph had been delighted with her room, its quaint copper roll-top bathtub, vast iron bedstead and panoramic loch view.

'Glen Muir Castle has been in Jack McGregor's family for generations. Have you had a full tour with Fraser yet?'

'Not the full tour, but what I have seen has been fabulous.' It wasn't every day you got the chance to explore a picturesque tower house castle on a loch. 'I can see why they fell for it. It's like something from a fairytale, but select, and not so opulent that it's offputting. It's like the best-kept secret getaway location in the Highlands.'

'We should add that to the brochure, you must tell Jack,' said Jess. 'I can see why you were good at your job in London. Jack, Fraser and Ally are brilliant bosses, I couldn't ask for better and I love working for them all.' Jess nodded to a large shield that bore the crest of the Clan McGregor. 'Jack's family emblem. Impressive, isn't it?'

Steph nodded in agreement. Jess was clearly a huge fan of all things McGregor.

'Right then, let's run through the bookings system, then we'll stop for a tea break.'

Steph grinned. 'I always perk up when anyone mentions tea.'

* * *

Jess poured tea and offered biscuits and delicious slabs of homemade Rocky Road in the comfortable staffroom that adjoined reception. 'So, you mentioned a bad experience — has man trouble led you here, then?'

Steph paused, wary of how much to reveal. Jess was certainly direct, but

Steph sensed she was just being interested and friendly. 'I had a busy job in London; it didn't leave much free time. There was a guy four years ago but since then work's been my focus. And now I don't even have work to fall back on. I feel as if I've been dropped from a great height; I'm still disorientated by life's changes, I suppose.'

She didn't want to go divulging details about her relationship with Charlie. Telling people your ex had died usually elicited sympathy and regret, which caused awkwardness, and she didn't want to go there. She certainly didn't want to explain her root feelings of anger and betrayal.

'So tell me about you,' she said as a diversion.

Jess laughed. 'Married young, cooked, cleaned, reared children, lived in the village all her life — The End.'

'You have what you want, and that's admirable — I've just lost all my life's good bits in a oner.'

'Then let me divert you by telling

you about Jack,' said Jess, winking meaningfully. 'He was featured in *The Scotsman's* eligible bachelor list, you know. Jack is a hero around here, local lad made good . . . isn't that even a tiny bit tempting?'

Steph shook her head. 'I think he has plenty of admirers without adding me as one more. One in particular by the name of Hilary springs to mind . . . '

Jess rolled her eyes. 'Thank goodness she's gone. She was chasing Jack down like he was a fox during hunting season.'

'I think she overstayed her welcome.'

'He can do a lot better than her.' Jess offered Steph more tea from the pot. 'Let me show you my wedding pictures — Jack was Gordon's best man, and he's little Blair and Lisa's godfather.' Jess reached into a locker and retrieved her cell phone, flicking through photographs.

'We had to get married quickly so it was a quiet, small affair. I sometimes wish I'd had a big, grand wedding like in all the glossy magazines but my grandmother had terminal cancer, you see, and all I wanted was for her to see me walk down the aisle. So we didn't save up for ages — we just went for it, to ensure that the ones we loved most were there.'

Steph was truly touched by the little glimpse into Jess's thinking and past hard emotional times.

She flicked through the photos and saw the kilted and smiling Jack, unmistakable with that handsome, dark head of hair, sharp eyes and tall gait; his attire of full dress kilt caused her tummy to flip over unbidden, but she vowed to take no heed.

Jess pointed out an attractive and chicly dressed brunette in a group photo next to him. 'May she never darken our doors again — nasty piece of work. All she cared about was money and status. Hilary was bad, but Paula Banning was much worse.'

The comment held significant resonance for Steph. It cut deeply, she knew, when someone claimed to care but had murkier motives that wrecked your trust . . . like Charlie.

Did Jack's heart carry such wounds, too?

But all she said aloud was, 'Who is she? They make a good-looking couple.'

'Jack's ex. They were engaged and Paula Banning acted quite the Laird's lady with her airs and graces, but she treated him badly and proved her lack of worth. She challenged the one thing that Jack holds dearest — his family — and it almost tore them all apart.'

Steph cleared her throat, uncomfortable to be gossiping about Jack's private affairs. 'It sounds as if he made a lucky escape, then, even if she is beautiful.'

'Paula was a looker, but she had a well-concealed heart of stone. She betrayed Jack in the worst way imaginable.'

'Show me these bonny bairns of yours,' Steph encouraged, changing the subject.

Jess showed a photo of two happy,

beaming children. Her smile was the picture of a mother's radiant pride.

'You're so lucky.'

'And so was Jack, to escape Paula Banning. Then again, another McGregor male wasn't so fortunate. Right. Tea break's over. Time to stop nattering and get back to the desk.'

★　★　★

The sight of Steph sitting on a bar stool in the hotel's Highlander Bar caused Jack something surprising — a warm, sharp surge of adrenaline and an inner peak of awareness. He hadn't felt that in a very long time. And for good reason, too.

Steph was smiling at him now. Wearing a turquoise sweater and white linen jeans, she looked better with every step closer he took. But Jack chastised himself for letting the hotel's latest distraction command his thoughts. He had enough on his plate without following attraction's fickle lead, no matter how attractive he may find Steph Baxter. Since Paula, women were out. He preferred his sanity intact and his heart out of harm's reach. Women couldn't be trusted. It would take a very special someone to ensnare a heart iced over by past hurts.

'Steph. You came.'

'Of course. I wouldn't dare turn down an official summons from the Laird of Glen Muir.' She gave a mock bow. 'Plus I needed a drink. I've just had my first hotelier's crash course and I'm still in recovery. It's hard work here, isn't it?'

He laughed as he perched on the stool beside her. 'Actually, I'm not the Laird — that's my dad — but I am the Laird's stand-in if that makes me sound more exciting. I didn't realise you were into titles.'

'Very exciting, but I'm not into titles at all. Unless it's on a good book or a wine bottle.' Steph laughed. 'Do I have to mind my Ps and Qs or follow special customs when I'm around you?'

He motioned to her glass to see if she wanted another drink, then ordered a sparkling water for himself. 'Just let me buy you a drink and be nice to me, that's all I ask. I'm easy to placate.'

He understood from Fraser that she'd come to Abercarrick to nurse wounds — he knew that feeling well.

In Steph's case it was a lost job, a change of flat; perhaps a broken heart? He'd overheard Jess mentioning how it was a pity that Steph was single when she was so pretty. He'd agreed, then quashed the thought. He'd recognised a tiny flicker of pleasure at that news, too. Jess had mentioned that Steph had been quite secretive about her affairs of the heart.

And now he had a proposition of his own.

Jack passed over the folder he'd brought. 'The file for the Highland fair. Speak to Murdo Stephenson, our groundsman, about the marquees but there's a full plan in the file. Should be fun. Shout if you need help. It's basically just trouble-shooting and rechecking timings and arrangements just before the event. Jess does the admin and Ally usually runs around on the day.'

Steph leafed through the pages and smiled. 'That's what I like to see. A client who's organised and efficient. Did you do this yourself or did you get one of your serfs to do it for you?'

'Jess is no serf. Let her hear you say that and it'll be a firing squad at dawn for you. Jess is my admin lifesaver. You should see my doctor's notes; I'm beyond hope.' Jack cleared his throat. 'Actually . . . I wondered if I could pick your brains . . . ?'

'So you didn't invite me to bill me for that wheel change? Wasn't sure I could afford doctor's rates.'

Jack felt his lips twitch with laughter again. She was good at deflecting with humour; he liked that, but sometimes he just wanted to get straight answers. He suspected she used her humour as a shield; those who joked the most were

41

the best at deflecting, he knew that from his dealings with patients.

And of course there was Hamish — the joker brother who'd played the ultimate unfunny surprise. Jack knew from experience that people could hide dark secrets behind a witty quip.

'I won't charge you. I'll just try to persuade you in other directions,' he replied with equal humour.

'Sounds ominous.'

'You're a qualified marketer, Fraser told me. Could you have a look at this?' He handed Hilary's effort over. 'It's a promotional and marketing plan. It recommends expansion opportunities and a promotional programme for widening our customer base.'

'I'll take a look. I may be redundant but I'm not completely rusty yet.'

Jack found himself staring at Steph; watching her neat, unpolished but smartly groomed fingernails and the light, glossy sheen on her lips. 'I won't prejudice your view by telling you what I think. I'll wait for your professional opinion.'

'Do you have a deadline?'

'No. But I need something to send to the bank soon. I'll take this one stage at a time.'

'I like a flexible customer. At least, I did when I had a job.'

'Hit you hard?' Jack asked, seeing her frown.

'I'm adjusting. Plus I haven't had time to mope since I arrived. The bosses here are mean taskmasters.'

'Well, there may be some future consultancy work here at Glen Muir. I may need marketing expertise and I'd be happy to pay for an informed opinion and redirect your talents. But we'll discuss it some other time once you've read this.' Jack looked deep into her grey eyes. They were mesmerisingly long-lashed. 'You've come to a good place to adjust, Steph. Glen Muir is good for the soul. Plus we have a great spa here — try any free treatment you fancy as therapy.'

'Honestly, Jack, you don't have to keep looking after me. A doctor, a laird

— how do you fit it all in?'

'Jack of all trades, master of none,' he told her, checking his watch. 'Shame I can't work out how to squeeze in more free time. I have to dash away again, I'm afraid. How about we meet up tomorrow at lunchtime? I'll drive you around the estate if you like, weather permitting.'

'I'd like that.'

Jack put down his empty glass. 'Go get your dinner — and be sure to sample the chocolate mousse. People flock here just for Fraser's top delicacy.'

He watched her leave and go into the dining room.

There was something about Stephanie Baxter — she was a hard woman not to become drawn to. Her looks, the dark curl of her amazing eyelashes, even that seed pearl choker against her sun-kissed skin . . .

But minor details like eyelashes and skin were strictly banned. There was only space for business — and for his father. He must tread more carefully.

But his conviction echoed hollowly in Jack's head — and his heart.

* * *

Dinner at Glen Muir was nothing short of a gastronomic feast. Fraser was an amazing chef — and he'd picked out a fabulous culinary team to support his vision. He had shunned his own Soho, London restaurant for Scottish country living proper. Ally's flair as an interiors guru had fuelled the inspiration for their castle escape. Going by the busy restaurant and impeccable service tonight, it was a wild plan that was paying off.

Steph was just finishing the café latte she'd chosen as a conclusion to her delicious dinner, when a waitress drew her aside to take a phone call.

'Steph. It's Ally, I can't talk for long. The nurses watch me like hawks,' the strident voice boomed from the receiver.

'Ally — how are you? I can't wait to see you — but keep your strength and

45

stay well for you and the baby.'

'That's why I'm calling. I'm going crazy in here and I want you to come and visit. You've to stock up on gossip magazines and as many crossword books as you can find. I was thinking Friday.'

'Ally, you should know better than to excite yourself.' Steph smiled wryly. 'Crossword books could be pushing it! Sounds like you're feeling better, then?'

'As better as I can be, alone and stuck in hospital, missing out on gossip and having fun with you. I called Jack already and he said he'd bring you on Friday.'

An alarm bell went off in Steph's head. 'Don't trouble Jack, he's busy enough.'

'It's already arranged and he didn't object.'

But maybe I would, she thought. *Can I handle a solo journey with the Laird of Glen Muir, his cheeky smile and glittering eyes?*

Especially now he was involving her

closely in his business too; she'd started reading the marketing report during dinner. It made interesting reading and now she realised that Jack McGregor did indeed need marketing help — in fact, he needed guidance urgently. Was she ready to work one-to-one with him?

She had no time to argue.

'Got to go! Here comes the sister.' And Ally hung up.

Steph wasn't entirely comfortable with the arrangement but what choice did she have? Jack had enough to do without being her chauffeur, but Ally wasn't good at taking no for an answer.

★   ★   ★

Steph had promised herself a brief walk around the grounds before bed but as she walked out into the dusky light outside Glen Muir, a startling sound caused panic to rise within her. Her hands began to sweat and her mouth went dry as a motorbike engine revved erratically in the distance.

The engine sounded wild; like a noisy and threatening insect that brought menacing ghosts back from her past. Raw panic seized Steph, immobilising good sense or reason or the ability to stop autopilot reactions. She scanned the horizon; the faint outline of a man on a bike, moving over hilly terrain in the distance, had her heart hammering a tattoo in her chest. She knew only that she had to stop him.

'Charlie! No!' She cried the words aloud, even though a lucid part of her brain told her it couldn't be.

Charlie was dead. She'd read the coroner's report. She'd seen the mangled wreckage of the flimsy scooter. The memory forced her into action and she let blind instinct lead her.

Steph turned, pivoting on her heels and running towards a woman now rounding the corner of the hotel building. The woman had a dog on a leash and Steph pleaded before she'd even reached her. 'We have to stop him. He's going to have an accident.'

'Whoa! Steph . . . what's up? It's me. It's Jess.'

Steph stared at her in anxious confusion. Jess, clad in jeans and a sweater, her expression pure puzzlement, accompanied by a dark brown retriever-type dog.

'Jess?'

'I always walk Phoenix down to the lochside at night.' Jess's face suggested Steph's appearance and the urgency in her voice had given her a jolt.

'There's someone on a motorbike. You have to stop him.'

Steph ran again, this time towards the biker, with Jess and her dog hot on her heels calling, 'Steph. It's only Jack. He's not in any danger. You seem freaked out — are you okay?'

The lone motorbike driver was turning speedy circles just as Charlie had done that night. He wasn't wearing a helmet; didn't he realise how foolhardy his behaviour was?

Steph pointed to the man on the bike who was getting closer. The sound of the thrumming engine buzzed and her breath caught as she remembered the heat of that night in Rhodes. The snarled annoyance on Charlie's face as she'd tried to persuade him out of his foolish actions.

'Don't go off in a mood like this,' she remembered saying.

He'd answered, 'You don't want me any more. Why do you care what I do, anyway?'

Steph blinked back the rush of panic and remorse at the memory and turned to Jess. How could she explain?

Looking up in anguish as the bike drew nearer, Steph could see that this wasn't a scooter at all; it was larger, with more wheels and a chunkier chassis.

Jess put her hand gently on her arm. Her tone was soothing. 'Steph, it's Jack. He's a seasoned quad biker and he always takes the bike out at night. He's won trophies. He won't have any mishaps. Why are you so scared?'

Steph immediately saw that the figure

was indeed Jack McGregor and the bike was a bulky quad bike. She turned as her own sense of foolishness thundered inside her, head spinning heart beating hard.

'I'm sorry, Jess. I made a mistake.'

The ghosts had tricked her. The dreams had blurred with reality. Nightmares in replay — but she'd got it wrong. Steph gulped back a sob and ran up the drive, leaving Jess staring after her.

What an idiot! She chided herself. *This isn't Greece, it's Scotland. And Charlie won't ever be coming back.*

★ ★ ★

Jess's tentative knock rapped softly on Steph's room door. Steph had been staring at the ceiling, reeling at the mini drama she'd just caused. How very wrong could she be?

'You okay? Steph, I'm worried about you. Let me in.'

Steph went to the door and opened it

a chink. She knew she must look a fright, with red-rimmed eyes and mangled hair, but keeping Jess out would only hurt her and cause more concern.

'I'm fine. I'm sorry I got in a state.'

Jess was holding a glass of amber-coloured liquid that she offered when the door opened wider. 'Medicinal brandy, as advised by Dr McGregor. He doesn't take no for an answer from his patients. Steph, you don't have to explain anything — you're in a strange place and we've been working you hard since you got here. It's unfair of us not to give you any space. Plus you've been worrying about Ally.'

Steph tried to hold back the tears that were threatening to fall at Jess's kindness. 'I got a bit confused. Where's Phoenix?'

'Jack's taken her for a run. Or maybe that's vice versa? He's great at throwing sticks but he'll tire before she does.'

Steph explained, 'If I'm honest I haven't been sleeping and that hasn't helped. Let's just say I had a bad experience on holiday once; my ex was in an accident and I'm not a fan of motorbikes. I suppose I just freaked out without thinking it through.'

Jess's expression was reassuring. 'No need to apologise or explain, just get a good night's rest. You sure you'll be okay on your own? I can stay if you'd rather?'

Steph shook her head and took the brandy glass and let a sip of its warming fire kindle inside her. 'Mmm, the good stuff, eh?'

'I only get good labels out for good friends,' Jess cajoled. 'Don't tell Fraser — he'd dock my wages!'

Steph knew she may be erratic at times and plagued by her past, but at least she had wonderful, caring friends around her in Abercarrick. She was lucky to be here.

She forced a smile. 'No wonder you're prized here, Jess. Thank you.'

Jess pulled her close for a hug. 'If you ever want to talk, I'm here. At Glen

Muir, our guests are family. And that's not just brochure-speak, it's true.' Her eyes reinforced the sincerity of her expression of empathy.

Grateful for the compassion, Steph drained her glass. Then she went to bed and for once, she slept. The brandy from Jack and Jess had done its job.

4

The next morning Steph sought Jess out and tried to explain in the simplest, most basic way she knew why she'd reacted as she had the night before.

After a deep breath she confided privately, 'The guy I loved died in an accident on a scooter. Four years ago now. It was complicated and I still get flashbacks. We'd grown apart when he died and I guess I still feel guilty about it.'

Jess had hugged her warmly and assured her that her private business would go no further.

Jess's frank and friendly dealings helped Steph forget the 'motorbike mistake' experience and put it behind her. The confidence also helped her realise that maybe a period of respite would do her a power of good.

Steph threw herself into preparations

for the Highland fair in earnest. After calling round all the main participants and talking to the grounds staff, she assured herself the plans were problem free and began to work through her own event checklist. After all the calls were complete and questions answered she finally felt she had a handle on the event.

The schedule for the fair would be busy, but it also promised to be a spectacle-filled, enjoyable day.

After a full morning of getting up to speed, she gave herself permission for a break to acquire Ally's requested magazine supplies. Donning her walking shoes and adding a rain jacket to her rucksack she set off in bright sunshine to find the local store in Strathinch, which lay along a wild and winding tree-lined lane.

The loch glimmered invitingly on one side of the track while on the other the hills were resplendent in majestic hues, flanked by dense pine forest. The scene was further brightened by yellow flag iris and purple rhododendrons in wild abundance.

The Strathinch General Store was supposed to be less than a half hour's walk away. Before long though, Steph wished she'd thought to bring insect repellent; the bloodthirsty midges were disturbing her tranquillity.

When Steph reached the shop, a beady-eyed cockerel appeared to be manning the old-fashioned fuel pumps that stood sentry outside it, crowing its belly out at visitors. Steph's heart upped tempo in shock when it surprised her with a lusty greeting but she laughed when she saw its proud posturing.

'Sorry to trespass,' she replied to its scowls.

A man appeared, watching her over the top of gold-rimmed glasses. 'Hello there. I'm Niven Reed, owner of the shop. You've come on foot — staying nearby?'

'Glen Muir Hotel.'

'Best in the region. Come on in.

Taking advantage of the sunshine, were you?'

'Absolutely.' Steph smiled. 'I only arrived yesterday, so I thought I'd get out and explore.'

Niven beckoned Steph inside his store, pointing out the highlights of his wares which included local guide-books and maps. Inside, the shop boasted a vast array of goods from everyday necessities to tourist bits and bobs, and Steph quickly set about picking up supplies.

'Hi,' said a familiar Scottish male voice from the other side of the store aisle.

The greeting made her heart speed almost as much as it had at the cockerel as Steph looked up into familiar, deep blue eyes and smiled. 'Hello, Jack.'

'Did I startle you?' Jack's gaze glittered like coal shards. There was an amused glint; he was ever the naughty boy and he used it to his advantage.

Steph replied, 'The noisy bird outside beat you hands down, although you always turn up when I least expect you, Jack.'

'Part of my charm?'

'Fishing for compliments?'

He grinned. 'As if I would. I'm here sorting out some orders with Niven. As to the cockerel, that's Roger. We should have warned you about him.'

'Roger?'

'Named after Roger Bannister, the runner. He does a mean sprint around the yard chasing off the cats. Niven swears he's better than a guard dog.' Humour danced in Jack's blue eyes and Steph laughed at the thought of a locally famous cockerel called Roger.

'There's a heart of gold under all those feathers,' Jack advised. 'You getting to know the local area? You should have said, I'd have given you Jack's Special Guided Tour. I know all the best secret places.'

Steph held up the guidebook she'd just selected. 'As delightful as that sounds, I wouldn't want to put you out, given your busy schedule, Dr McGregor. You might get called away on an emergency.' Steph smiled. 'I'm here under orders to get magazines for Ally and I daren't disappoint her; she's scary when incarcerated.'

'It's a hospital, not prison.'

'Try telling that to always-at-the-epicentre Ally.'

Jack circled the aisle to come and stand beside her. Up close he was tall, dark and glowing with vigour and health. He smelled of something woodsy and fresh with a hint of citrus and he looked shower-fresh. His faded jeans and a downy-soft polo shirt made him all the more approachable. Earthy and rugged sprang to mind as perfect descriptors for Glen Muir's heir and leader.

'Hey Jack,' a burry voice behind the post office counter said. 'Don't tell me you're bad-mouthing Roger again?'

Jack turned to greet Niven.

'I'm explaining his legendary status. One day there'll be a blue plaque out there beside the pumps with his name on it. Have you met Steph yet?'

Proper introductions were duly made

to both Niven and his wife, Hazel, who set about making up a complimentary fruit and chocolates gift basket for Steph to take to Ally when she learned about her hospitalisation.

'Can I assist you with anything else?' Niven asked helpfully.

'All done, thanks. I came to seek out Steph.' Jack's voice was soft and smoky as she felt his eyes rest on her. 'Can I give you a lift back to Glen Muir?'

'That'd be great. The views were lovely and the walk was nice but I don't want to encourage more insect bites. Which reminds me; I should buy cream to slay them while I'm here.'

Niven went off to fetch repellent and Hazel made chit-chat with Steph, offering tips on places to visit and things to try during her stay. 'The midges are a local hazard. Some locals swear by vinegar,' Hazel explained.

Steph replied wryly, 'I'm working at the hotel for a while during Ally's hospitalisation and I'm not sure Eau de Chip Shop would be appreciated by five-star guests.'

From behind her, the low, earthy rumble of Jack's laughter made her turn. His eyes danced as he smiled at her.

'You planning on driving my guests away? Speak to the spa about citronella. You don't need to go bathing in Fraser's condiments just yet. Of course, far be it from me to dissuade you. I like a good fish supper as much as the next man.'

Jack pushed a hand through his hair and Steph found herself admiring the way the dark, thick strands had a hint of curl. The attractive line of his shoulders through his shirt were clearly visible when he turned to talk to Niven.

She heard Niven mention Australia as he handed Jack a letter. Jack's face looked grim as he perused it. Steph only noticed because it was utterly at odds with his usual easy manner and Steph found herself wondering what was up. She'd likely never know. She swiftly pulled herself together, then excused herself and went to find what she needed on the magazine stand, then paid at the counter.

When they left together, it was with assurances from the owners that they were looking forward to the Highland fair and were geared up for a charity tombola.

'So what did you want me for?' Steph asked, noticing that Jack had folded the letter and pocketed it unread.

'To make sure I can still take you to see Ally tomorrow? And of course to apologise. I'm sorry I scared you last night. In retrospect it was foolhardy. I've been teaching a local lad how to use his quad bike. Next time we'll do it well out of earshot of the hotel.' Looking at her levelly he said, 'I wanted to say sorry and ask you if you'd join me for dinner tonight.'

His beseeching look made her tummy tilt and turn, but Steph smiled and shook her head. 'No need to apologise, Jack. You really don't have to do anything.'

'But I want to,' insisted Jack,

watching her. 'You're helping out in the hotel. You're new here and it's not every day I get the chance to give the local gossip mill a field day. I'll get to go out and eat great food with a beautiful woman for company. You'll up my cool cred no end.'

Steph felt her cheeks glow crimson at the attention, which was crazy. The man was just being nice, and all the locals had a warm, welcoming manner. Why should Jack McGregor's be any more than local hospitality and friendship?

'Shouldn't the local doctor be more conservative in his behaviour?' She faked a prim look. 'Encouraging gossip just to wind the locals up?'

Jack narrowed his eyes. 'I like to live dangerously. I've always had rebel tendencies.'

Steph shrugged then nodded. 'Then since you're being wild and reckless, I'll have to make sure you don't go loco. I'm not going to say no to dinner with Fraser's business partner or the Laird's son.'

'And here was me hoping you'd like to go out with 'just Jack'.' Jack paused and looked off into the distance. 'I'd like to take you somewhere different. Off premises since you're spending so much time working. And anyway, this way you can experience some local flavour. Guidebooks are great but there's nothing like hands-on experience.'

Steph grinned. Energy and excitement always seemed to bubble inside her like heady champagne when Jack was around. 'Sounds mysterious, but nice. I'd like that.'

They simultaneously noticed that small droplets of rain had started to patter down.

'Rain.' Steph grimaced.

'Do you think when we're together we bring it on?' He re-ran the firecracker smile, only this time with full orchestral accompaniment. 'We'll have to hide out in my car again.'

She nodded. Steph knew that in seconds her hair was going to be in damp strands, her jacket would be wet through and droplets would be running a race down her back.

They ran to the silver sports car and, getting inside, she smelled Jack's familiar citrus scent.

'So dinner tonight is on. It'll be a new experience — you'll like it.' Jack drummed his thumbs on the steering wheel. He regarded her with deep, dark eyes that made her mouth go dry.

Steph pulled back damp strands of hair as he started the car. 'Are you avoiding telling me where on purpose?'

'A dash of mystery does no harm when you're trying to impress and it'll be worth the wait, I assure you. I'll meet you in the bar at seven thirty.'

'Okay, boss.'

'Tonight I'm not the boss. We're friends who're getting to know each other better.' Jack's gaze was earnest and searching. One brow rose in a way that told her he meant it.

'Okay. I'll go with the flow. I'm at your mercy.'

'If only,' he answered in a flirty way that buoyed her inside.

He drove in silence and pretty soon they were nearing Glen Muir again. Steph reflected that Jack wasn't hitting on her, and she should calm down her thrumming pulse.

He was just opening the way to being business colleagues and friends. She should welcome that. She really must stop herself questioning motives or getting quite so jittery when she imagined there was chemistry. She should accept that he was a charming man and this was his forte.

Especially since she was off men and the last thing she needed was a dalliance in Scotland with a man so connected to her friends' futures; a man with more than enough on his plate.

But in spite of inner affirmations, Steph found herself watching his strong hands as he worked his way up through the gears and rain flew across the windscreen in sheets of clear liquid. They reached the hotel quickly and he drove to the entrance to save her from getting soaked.

With the car at a standstill he turned in his seat. 'I want to get to know you better, Steph, and tonight I intend to do that.'

For a moment she felt an undeniable frisson of chemistry. Was this just friendship, or more? Was she imagining it?

She pulled the door lever. 'Do you plan on wearing a dinner suit tonight?'

'Do you have a thing for me in the posh look, then?'

'I'm checking since I don't know where we're going. I'm not asking you to wear it for me, I just need to know if I have to dress up.' His comment had made her blush, feeling foolish.

'I'm sure you'll look wonderful in whatever you choose.' Jack's boyish grin caused an atomic explosion in Steph's head. Frankly, it sent tremors of delight up her every nerve ending.

'I'll wear it if you want me to — just say the word — but you have to wear a dress in return.' Jack's expression told her he was teasing her and he went on, 'Don't worry. I'll be low-key smart-but-casual. Though I quite fancy seeing you dressed up.'

'Charming.'

'I meant I'd like to see you out of that hotel uniform.'

'Jack. Stop before you put your foot in your mouth any further,' she said.

Underneath her faked calm, her mind was spinning and her mouth had gone dry.

She opened the door and climbed out into the rain, ready to run into the hotel. 'See you tonight. No tuxedo.'

'Looking forward to it.'

In a secret corner of her heart, Steph knew, so was she.

5

When Jack sped off, Steph realised the dynamic really was as potent as she'd believed. There was something in his eye contact; something that made her heart race and her pulse skitter. She was sure he felt it, too. So, how was she going to handle that tonight? Back off; encourage; ignore? She was as baffled as she was blown away by it all.

When she reached reception, Jess stood watching her with hands on hips and an accusing look in narrowed eyes.

'Hmmm. Getting chummy with Dr McGregor?' Jess gave a meaningful lift of her eyebrows.

Steph dismissed the comment. 'A lift in the rain, actually.'

'I knew there would be sparks. I just knew it.'

'What a vivid imagination you have. You're as bad as Ally.' Steph acted unfazed. 'I'd best get back to work. Lots to do. Busy, busy. Best keep the bosses on side.'

'Looks like you've succeeded pretty well with one of them already,' Jess muttered — just loudly enough for her to hear.

Unfortunately Steph now had other things on her mind. Like what to wear and how to act for their dinner date — and why the butterflies had taken up residence in her tummy whenever Jack smiled or flirted.

The matter of where on earth she was going to source a dress in a matter of hours, was at that moment, an epic and unsolvable mystery.

★　★　★

Two hours later Steph still didn't have a dress for her evening — but she had unearthed something far more exciting for Glen Muir Hotel.

She'd gone to find the citronella Jack had told her about in the hotel's spa

71

just after she'd read Hilary Benson's management-speak, buzzword-loaded marketing report earlier.

It was very poor; unimaginative and uninformed, especially given what she imagined the woman must have charged to drive the car she'd sped off in a huff in.

But it *had* created a spark in Steph and her ideas had begun on a slow burn, building up gradually in her mind until she felt quite excited by the whole prospect.

She could help; thinking about how she would market Glen Muir, how she could enhance its profile her way, improve its marketing strategy and make it the shining diamond in the Highlands that it so richly deserved to be.

She found herself standing in the spa's reception being greeted by the lovely lady who ran it. Steph procured the citronella essential oil, then having introduced herself and discovered that the woman's name was Shona, Steph decided to do some detective work of her own.

'I'm actually a friend of Ally and Fraser's and I'm doing some work for Jack. I don't suppose I could ask some questions?'

'I'd welcome it, but right now is a bit busy with back-to-back clients. How about you drop by tomorrow, or book a treatment sometime? A pedicure is great for talking. Massages aren't so good — most people fall fast asleep.'

'That sounds divine. The pedicure, I mean.'

Steph booked herself the treatment for a few days ahead — with the fair to work on, maybe now wasn't the best time to be diving straight into marketing strategising. She would plan a raft of questions and come prepared.

Steph nodded to Shona's obvious baby bump. 'Looks like you and Ally are baby buddies.'

'My due date is three weeks after hers. How is Ally?'

'Much better,' she replied. 'And getting good care.'

Shona smiled. She was so calm and

serene, a perfect spa employee. Steph decided to launch in with one of her ideas.

'As a newcomer to the area, what do you think of this idea, Shona . . . would it be feasible to produce tiny vials of these oils for insect bites, as freebies for guests' rooms? It might alert guests who haven't used the spa to its exist-ence. How would you feel about me suggesting it to Jack?'

Shona nodded. 'There would be a cost implication, but it wouldn't be much. It would be a good advert for the spa — perhaps accompanied by a discount voucher?'

'Great thinking. We're on the same wavelength. So you think it could work?'

'Definitely,' said Shona. 'And I know Jack's keen to boost the spa's potential if it's possible. We run on a limited staff at the moment but I'm sure we could do so much more.'

As Steph left, her eyes strayed to a cabinet of items displayed in the spa foyer — a local soap company touting its wares, its handmade soaps and tinctures a local speciality.

Thick blocks of edible-looking hand-made soaps full of wonderful natural ingredients, from bog myrtle to heather. The thought of bathing in them had her yearning for a soak. They were piled high in baskets like pastel-coloured confectionery slabs.

'Do you use these?' Steph asked.

'We encourage local enterprise. They're a great outfit; terrific treatments, too. Their masks and creams are luxurious — try a sample if you like and I'll give you a leaflet with their blurb.'

Steph accepted the freebies keenly. It was just a hunch, but right now she figured some of the answers Hilary had so clearly missed had been right under her nose, in the spa of all places. How on earth had the woman managed to miss the goldmine potential beneath her designer shoes in the Glen Muir hotel?

* * *

'Can we talk?' Steph asked, as she poked her head around the door of the large hotel kitchen.

Trying to get Fraser's attention in the midst of this gastronomic cabaret was no easy task. The bright lights and industrial chrome appliances acted as a backdrop for industrious culinary theatre. It looked like chaos, but smelled mouth-watering and Fraser motioned to Steph to enter and sit.

'I need to ask a favour,' she said, perching on his bench.

'Shoot.' Fraser swiftly plated up a dozen delicious-looking chocolate desserts, then wiped his hands and leapt from that task to the next.

'I need something to wear. Jack and I are eating out to discuss the fair plans. I don't want to look like a slouch in the trio of jeans I brought with me,' Steph said, biting her lip. 'Any chance I could borrow something from Ally's pre-pregnancy wardrobe? She always liked to dress up better than me,' she confessed, adding, 'And how is she?'

'Much improved,' Fraser reassured her. 'Having an enforced rest is doing her a power of good. Says she's enjoying the break from me — can you believe it?' Fraser pulled a mock expression of shock. 'And of course you can help yourself to clothes. Ally can't fit into them for a while anyway, and she won't mind. How are you getting on with Jack?'

'He's very committed to the business. And he's asked me for some marketing ideas. I'm hoping we'll discuss it later.'

Steph reeled off a number of questions about Glen Muir that she'd been wondering about relating to the spa, group bookings, advertising and the vacant buildings she'd seen in the estate grounds during that morning's walk. They'd looked like stables; she had a few ideas brewing about future potential for them.

'Are you getting enough help with the fair?'

'It's in hand. No need to worry.'

'Jack's the best business partner I

could have asked for — totally reliable and capable. Just shout if you need info or help.'

Suddenly Steph found her mind drifting off to the man that seemed to be the centre of everyone's conversations. Dark hair, expressive features, shoulders that held clothes as they should be worn and hinted at a strongly defined muscular frame.

What was it about him that got to her so? One smile and she lost control of her faculties.

Her imagination flitted back to when he'd untangled her bracelet from her hair by the fireside. The touch of skin on skin as the fire crackled and warned of hot chemistry, the electric adrenalin that had coursed through her veins at his proximity.

Steph shoved thoughts of Jack McGregor far, far away to a dark recess of her brain and was suddenly aware that Fraser was watching her intently.

'You okay? We're not pushing you too hard? This was supposed to be a break, not a working holiday.'

'Absolutely fine . . . Fraser, I was wondering . . . ' Steph said tentatively, trying to find the right words. 'Do you do much advertising here? You know, Sunday supplements and press ads? Do you have a big marketing budget?'

'Not as much as we should do.' He pushed a chocolate bowl and spatula towards her with a gesture that said *start licking*. It smelled fabulous and looked so tempting that she wanted to dive right in. 'A couple of regular ads. Jack's in charge of promotion mainly. What's on your mind?'

Hilary Benson's report was still in her thoughts. She hadn't been at all impressed, and it had made her think long and hard about solutions that were more far-reaching. She'd wanted to ask Fraser a few questions before she started committing her ideas to paper — or before she spoke them aloud with Jack.

Steph had a distinct feeling that Fraser and Ally had gone to town so much on the things they loved, the restaurant and the renovation, that they'd overlooked promotion and the spa, as well as other opportunities for increasing income.

Steph replied casually, 'If I were to think over some suggestions for upping your advertising, would you let me discuss them with you?'

'It's your area of expertise, but you'd have to run them past Jack too, of course — though we haven't much of a budget. That's part of the problem, cash is seriously committed.'

Steph sighed. 'I won't do anything firm without your say-so and I'll stay low key.'

★ ★ ★

Back in her room, Steph studied her reflection long and hard.

She'd rifled through Ally's clothes and in the end she plumped for a smart French navy wrap-around dress in a soft, silky, shimmering fabric worn with her own heeled, red knee-high boots. It had a flattering neckline but wasn't too fussy, nor did it smack of too much effort. It felt dressed-up but casual; just right.

Her hair gleamed and fell about her shoulders in the way a newly washed mane should. She brushed on lip-gloss and was liberally spraying on some scent when a rap at the door made her heart jump.

Surprisingly she found Jack McGregor standing outside. He looked sensational, and she inwardly dismissed her fixation on his dinner suit attire. He was dressed in a pale blue shirt worn with a smart slate-grey suit. How could any man be so effortlessly handsome and dashing with such laid-back ease? As dinner dates went, she'd won the lottery.

'Hi — weren't we meeting in the bar?' she queried.

'I thought maybe we should keep this discreet. Tongues wag if you let them. We can go out the back way and then the staff won't notice.'

Steph faked a wary look. 'Ashamed of me now?' she jibed.

Jack gave her a dark, earnest look. 'Dressed like that, I don't think so. You look amazing. Didn't you see my jaw drop and roll across the floor?'

'Flattery will get you everywhere.' Steph picked up her clutch bag. 'I've been a busy girl today. Researching Hilary's findings. I have thoughts to impart. For example — '

Jack put up a warning finger. 'As delighted as I am to hear it, may I remind you that this is purely social?'

'Oh, right — of course, if you say so.'

Steph frowned. In truth she felt slightly chastened, and he must have read as much from her look because he added, 'As much as I'm sure your ideas are fantastic and I can't wait to hear your findings.'

She'd actually been feeling elated and now that the ideas had started coming in earnest she couldn't wait to share them. Glen Muir had such potential and tapping it was an exciting opportunity; for her and hopefully for its owners. With the right tweaks this place could be so very much more.

Steph pushed her euphoria down and willed her pulse to regulate. 'Okay. Dinner. Shall we go?'

'Definitely. That dress is sensational,' he remarked. 'Glad I insisted on glamming you up.'

'So, where are you taking me?'

'All in good time.'

The butterflies in her stomach spun into a flurry and she tried to keep her excitement contained. The look in his eyes and the scent of his cologne was enough to put all her senses on high alert.

'I brought you this,' Jack said, handing over an umbrella. It was white and pink and bore a painted border of clusters of Scottish thistles. It was very touristy, but girly too. 'I would've got the matching Wellington boots but I didn't know your size. Tell me and I'll get them to match.'

Steph regarded him quizzically. 'Expecting a downpour?'

'We should be prepared, especially

since we keep encountering rainstorms together.'

They held each other's gaze, briefly enjoying the view before shyness crept up and tapped Steph gently on the shoulder.

'C'mon — let's go or we'll miss our reservation,' Jack encouraged, cupping her elbow as he led her out towards her mystery evening tryst.

6

Beachcomber's Cove wasn't just off the beaten track; it was the region's hidden gem and Jack McGregor's own secret private treasure. The food wasn't flashy, or award-winning like Fraser's — just local, good quality, hearty fare and fresh seafood made and served with love.

It was the ambience and location that were its magical allure. It wasn't an architectural marvel of a building either — just a low-key timber beach shack made more robust and permanent with a glass-enclosed deck terrace where diners could marvel at the rolling waves, crystal waters and shimmering silver sands.

To some it may be a beach bum of a restaurant, but to Jack McGregor it was paradise found.

Would Steph Baxter agree? Was he crazy to care? Especially when it was a place with so many mixed memories. A place that had been regularly frequented when he'd been part of a couple; where he'd first set eyes on Paula.

Jack swiftly pushed his thoughts away and wondered briefly if he'd misjudged himself. Maybe he wasn't as 'over' things as he'd thought?

But Steph deserved a treat. He'd stayed out of her way after the motorbike incident, but he'd known from what Jess had told him that his actions had upset her deeply, and that bothered him. Clearly she'd suffered some trauma in the past, and while he wouldn't probe — it wasn't his place — he could make amends and offer the hand of friendship.

Getting out of the car, he circled it and opened the door for Steph. A glimpse of her legs in those funky boots and that figure-hugging dress sparked a flare of excitement inside him, but the attraction wasn't something he cared to follow up on.

While he definitely felt the tug of Steph's allure, it was only hormones; a natural response to an attractive woman, the starry night and beach location.

It was the look of pure excitement and pleasure when she looked at him with her honest grey eyes that sent his heart racing fully and told him, no — this wasn't just an ordinary hormonal reaction. Immediately he knew she was the reason why he'd chosen to come here.

Steph marvelled at what was before her, leaning on the car park railing to take it in. She gasped and stared at him, which made him smile. Jack locked the car and then pointed out the twisting beach pathway.

'Like it?' Jack asked.

'I love it. It's spectacular.'

'Watch your step; the path is just shingle and sand and those boots have high heels — why don't you take my arm?'

As he watched her, the sea breeze lifted her hair like a cloud of sandy velvet and her dress shimmered and billowed behind her, like a mermaid princess come to land.

'You come here often?'

Jack smiled. 'Actually I do. Often on my own, that is. Their mussels and langoustines are fantastic — plus the owners are good personal friends.'

'You're the local doctor, Jack. You're friends with everyone and no one has a bad word to say about you — at least not in my hearing they haven't.'

'Depends who you speak to. Can't please everyone.'

If only she knew. Perhaps she should ask his brother! In truth he hadn't spoken to Hamish since his bombshell departure and Hamish hadn't ever seen any reason to look back. The pair had now reached an impasse that could never be bridged and that pained him.

Ordering himself not to spoil the evening by brooding, Jack linked his arm into Steph's.

'Wow,' she gasped. 'It's so pretty.'

'It's basic, but rather special, in my view.'

A tiny wooden structure stood proud

above an idyllic stretch of beach at the bottom of the path. Simple tea lights twinkled on every table. From a distance it was a fairytale, magical lair.

Inside, the floor was roughly sanded and the tables were sea-washed wood with assorted, mismatched chairs. Against this humble backdrop stout silver cutlery and crystal glasses gleamed. Fisherman's float lights dangled from rafter ropes but there were no table cloths, and no ceremony. Just a warm welcome, and a beguiling ocean view centre stage.

There was something other-worldly about it that always warmed Jack through.

'Hi, Manuel. You're well?' Jack greeted the owner warmly.

'Never better. You'll be pleased to hear my cholesterol levels have never been so good, thanks to Rhona's eagle eye.'

'See what you can do with stricter rules?'

They were steered by Manuel and his pretty wife Rhona to their reserved table.

Jack did brief introductions for Steph and was gratified to see her eyes sparkle as she gazed around at her surroundings. Her lightly glossed lips gleamed in the candlelight and he ached to reach out and touch her.

'Worth the wait?'

'You're a man of hidden talents. It's wonderful.'

'I'm glad. So no work talk. Just a chill out with unfussy Scottish dining. It's good to let your hair down — and by the way, yours is beautiful this evening.'

A tinge of blush painted Steph's cheeks. 'So many compliments, my head will get big.'

'Honestly given.'

'To your satisfaction, Dr Mac?' Manuel asked, returning to them with menus and a grin on his face at Steph's expression. 'Best seats in the house for you, Dr Mac, my best customer, and complimentary wine this evening, I think.' He glanced sidelong at Steph with a smile. 'I'll bring you a nice bottle of champagne, yes?'

'Only for my guest, I'm driving, but thank you, Manuel.' Jack nodded and removed his jacket. He wanted to savour and enjoy.

Manuel turned to Steph and said with loaded pride, 'He's the best doctor in the whole of Scotland, and our favourite customer. I'm so proud that he brings his lovely lady here when he has a grand castle at his disposal. What can I get for you this evening?'

Jack chose not to mention that Steph wasn't 'his lady' and Steph didn't object. Though he did observe her hesitant glance.

'What's on tonight's specials board? I've been looking forward to eating here all day,' Jack declared enthusiastically.

★　★　★

Jack McGregor was nothing if not surprising — this place, the view, the furnishings. There was a rowing boat in one corner and an oar and an old net full of shells as wall art. It was quirky, cobbled together, but it was also breathtaking. Steph couldn't help but adore Beachcomber Cove.

A tiny part of her admitted to herself that this was one of the most romantic locales she'd ever been taken to. It was certainly a stark contrast to Charlie's high-class restaurant habit.

And then, of course, there was the man himself; Jack.

She'd seen a few women diners turn to watch his easy strides to their table. They'd appreciated the view — and not of the seashore. She was so glad she'd dressed up and was feeling well turned out as it gave her more confidence.

Over a meal of seared trout and salad with a glass of bubbly for Steph and seafood platter with linguine for Jack, they discussed their lives in general.

'So, redundancy and the fact that Ally and Fraser are old friends aside, why did you come up here?' Jack asked twirling his fork in his pasta.

'Change of scene. To be honest,' Steph confided, 'I've been itching to break free of the city and the redundancy just sealed it, I suppose. Don't get me wrong, London's great, even if the Tube fares can be crippling and my tiny flat's at the far end of a Tube line because of cost, but sometimes you yearn for space.

'Plus my landlord's just found a buyer for my flat and I have just two months to move. I needed a brief respite — and you don't get much more rural than Glen Muir.'

'True.' Jack smiled. 'But too rural for you, perhaps?'

'No, just different. I'm used to readily available chain stores and wi-fi and a cappuccino on every corner. I'm not a retail junkie but let's just say I'm acclimatising. It's beautiful here, though; the air is fresh and clean and even the stars look brighter somehow. Does that sound daft?'

Jack was smiling at her strangely. 'That's because they are. Light pollution obscures them. And if you're into frothy coffees you can have one — I do a mean cappuccino; learned a trick or two in Italy — and Glen Muir can meet your city demands. So you're a material girl after all?'

'Far from it. I was born in Wales; Mum and Dad still live and run a business in Abergavenny. They own a knitting shop. I only moved to London to get my marketing degree, then it seemed sensible to stay and find work. That's how I met Ally and Fraser. Ally and I once shared a flat together.'

'That sounds like double trouble!' Jack's expression showed he was teasing.

'You wouldn't believe half the stories. We had fun together.'

'Maybe we'll have to schedule another night so you can give me the gory details?'

'That would be too incriminating. What happens between girls stays between girls.'

Another night together. It sounded good. If premature.

Steph savoured her delicious food before attempting to turn the attention back to Jack. 'So tell me about how you've ended up running a hotel and being the local GP? Do you just like making life hard for yourself or have you a split personality?'

Jack laid down his cutlery and sipped his water. 'Well, we've had to take on new responsibilities and obligations recently. I'm making the best of things, but sometimes it's hard going . . . '

He faltered, then added, 'You see, my dad's in a care home; he has dementia. Dealing with his care has certainly brought fresh challenges.'

'I'm so sorry. That was crass of me.' Steph instinctively reached out her hand to touch his, and her ring clattered against her glass. Jack righted it and swiftly took her fingers.

'It's okay. No offence taken. Life can be hard but all you can do is get on with it.' He smiled reassuringly and sat back.

'So is the 'we' you referred to you and your brother?'

Jack's gaze stayed on their joined

fingers. 'No. Hamish isn't in the picture these days, but I do have a little sister.' His tone mellowed as he went on, 'Marnie was once a pretty successful model, but now she's a beautician working in the Caribbean on a cruise ship, saving the world one mani/pedicure at a time.'

'And you're coping with all this on your own?'

'I have no choice. Plus, I am the doctor in the family.'

'But that shouldn't mean you inherit all the problems.'

'At first I thought he was just getting forgetful — he always had his own idiosyncratic quirks. But then it was more than just memory lapses. He was wandering away without telling anyone, even during the night . . . getting on buses with no clue where he was going . . . Then the aggression started and the confusion started to change his personality.

'Luckily the neighbourhood is filled with spies who alerted me to the problems — and people are generally really supportive and caring.'

'That still must have been a hard blow for you.'

'My mother died of a stroke ten years ago and Hamish moved abroad. Although going into business with Ally and Fraser was a just a detour at the time, they have great vision. Even though times are hard for everybody in business right now, it's working well. And it's good for me to know I'm keeping Dad's estate ticking along in my own way, now he can no longer do it for himself.'

Jack let go of her fingers and somehow she found herself missing the contact.

'From what Ally and Fraser have told me, they both agree they're lucky to have you,' she said. 'They're ardent supporters. As are most people in Glen Muir, Jack. You have a lot of friends on your side.'

'But prior to my getting involved in the hotel, Ally and Fraser were badly let down.'

Steph frowned, puzzled; she didn't

know what Jack was referring to.

His jaw clenched. 'My brother talks a good case but sometimes there's no substance. I chose to make the investment myself when I realised what was going on. Initially he was involved in negotiations with Ally and Fraser, but things went adrift and I had to step in.'

Steph sensed there was much more to the story but she didn't want to push or intrude into Jack's private family affairs. Now wasn't the time for interrogation but the new knowledge still came as a surprise, as Ally and Fraser had never made her privy to this news.

'There's not a day goes by when I don't regret that my father has to be looked after in a care home environment. I think about it often. I'm also sad that my brother isn't here because Dad worshipped him. But I know that while it may not be the preferred option on a personal level, it is the safest one for him. He has excellent care and dedicated supervision that I can't give him. I have obligations to my practice and the estate.'

'You've been through a lot, by the sounds of it.'

'Our family has weathered storms but we've got through them. Don't all people have to deal with life's unexpected slings and heart-breaking arrows?'

Steph sipped her drink and nodded, agreeing inwardly with what Jack had said.

She hadn't just known of such experiences — she'd lived them and loathed it. Charlie's high-handed ways, his denial, his insistent selfish agenda with scant regard for the relationship he was destroying in the process.

While these thoughts assailed her, Steph was unwilling to commit her experiences to words. Eventually, pushing sharp memories aside, she said, 'There's a saying; what doesn't kill you makes you stronger. It's true, but what it doesn't cover is that sometimes the heart takes a long time to recover.'

'Very true. You've been there too, then?'

'You could say that.'

Jack stared out to sea. 'Life can be very beautiful but sometimes it's more treacherous than you can cope with. A bit like that beautiful but wild sea out there.' He motioned to the rolling white-crested waves.

'Sometimes if you knew what lay beneath,' Steph added, 'you'd never have the courage to paddle at all.'

She knew that now would probably be a good time to offer insights into her motorbike fright; to explain about Charlie. Yet something held her back.

Sometimes the feelings inside felt like a maelstrom hidden beneath a sometimes calm, sometimes choppy surface. One little word would blow her cover and her emotional veneer of calm and then she feared it would all flood out, obliterating any composure and bringing back the ugly truth. She didn't want Jack to share that — and she didn't want Charlie marring this magical evening.

Charlie Hughes hadn't left her a broken woman; he'd left her wounded and emotionally mute. Psychological self-protective padding was all she could manage these days. Would she ever feel safe enough to swim in the sea of her emotions again?

'Dessert? Since I've dampened the mood like a lead-filled balloon,' Jack offered, breaking into her reflections with that dashing but intrinsically comforting smile.

'Just coffee, thanks. And then you can tell me if it's true that being a dashing doctor is a prescription for female attention?'

7

When Jack looked up, he knew immediately his evening with Steph was about to hit a downward curve. One minute they'd been talking about surgery life and he'd been revealing the highs and the occasional low points of his work — the next, *she* was walking in and he knew by the sharp flinch in his gut that there would be repercussions.

Virginia Johnson had a knack for referring pointedly to the times from his past which he chose to skirt round. She also had a bent towards revenge; hence his usual tactic of avoiding her.

Unfortunately she'd chosen tonight to dine here too and the size of the restaurant meant there was little room for evasion. She still held a mean grudge and he knew she would relish a spot of vitriolic taunting.

'Are you okay?' Steph asked. 'You've

gone quiet on me.'

The brightness of her smile made him feel bad for his own misgivings.

Jack laid down his coffee cup and napkin, and drew out his wallet even though he hadn't requested the bill yet. 'I'm fine. A touch of headache, actually. Do you mind if we head off? We could go back to the bar at Glen Muir.'

If he could get them out of there, all might still be well.

'We both have early starts and we're going to see Ally tomorrow so maybe that's a good plan,' Steph offered. 'If tomorrow's bad for you, I can make other arrangements.'

'I'll take you, not a problem. A paracetamol and I'll be fine. But I think you're right — time to head off.'

With an inward groan Jack was aware that Virginia had caught sight of him. His thoughts darkened and his head throbbed but it wasn't migraine; it was a pre-emptive reaction to seeing Paula's one-time best friend.

Virginia had been their nominated

bridesmaid at the wedding that never took place. And he knew through the grapevine that she'd been visiting in Australia within the last month.

If Steph hadn't been there, he'd have bolted for home.

'Hello, stranger.' Virginia's voice reached him before she did. Hardly surprising, given that it could shatter glass. 'Fancy seeing you here.'

Jack really didn't need an inquisition. He signalled to Manuel for the bill and laid notes, plus a generous tip, at the ready, but he knew it was too late.

'What brings you here? New girl-friend?' Virginia began with a personal probe.

He purposefully ignored it. 'Steph and I are good friends.'

'Speaking of friends — I'm back from Sydney, as you'll have gathered. Of course you've never gone yourself. They're very settled now,' she announced. 'It's such a glorious place — look at my tan! I really didn't want to leave.'

'Maybe you should emigrate? I

104

thought the golden glow was fake and hastily applied. Like your sincerity.'

Steph looked at him sharply and Jack immediately regretted his knee-jerk response.

Virginia's mouth puckered with obvious rage and inwardly he congratulated himself on a direct hit, even if he did feel like a louse for looking so petty in front of the woman he'd hoped to impress. She'd likely think he was obnoxious in the extreme.

After all, Steph had no idea of the truth — that Virigina had not only been bridesmaid for the wedding that never happened, but she'd also been the messenger girl, delivering Paula's bombshell note with a smile and much relish. Oh, she'd acted the concerned part, but he'd found out that every detail in it had been broadcast via the community tom-toms.

Paula had never given him the courtesy of a face-to-face explanation, and she'd picked the local gossip as her messenger — nice touch.

'Play nice, Jack,' Virginia purred insincerely. 'You know I wanted to put your feelings first. I would have if you'd listened to me, and we might've avoided you turning into the bitterest bachelor in town.'

She turned to Steph with obvious glee. 'I wouldn't waste your efforts, dear. He's damaged goods. If I couldn't catch him, I don't give you much hope.'

'Let's go, Steph,' Jack said softly, bile rising inside him, his urge to shove Virginia off the jetty and leave her to the mercy of the tides stronger than ever.

'Leaving so soon?' Virginia was now standing right beside their table. She was with a friend he hadn't even noticed; the mannequin type that totally missed Jack's radar.

He pulled on his jacket then took Steph's hand in his. 'We want to be alone. Sometimes company just isn't very palatable.'

* * *

'I'm detecting a bit of an old feud burning bright. I haven't made things bad for you, have I? She's not some vexed ex, is she?' Steph followed Jack up the twisting sandy path and continued, 'I mean, I don't mind being your foil, pretending to be your love interest for an old girlfriend or whatever, but it seems as if you're suddenly at war with the whole world. And me.'

'Just angry at her deplorable behaviour, which incidentally is nothing new. She's not an old girlfriend, Steph. Women like Virginia can't see past their own egos; other people's feelings don't count with the likes of her.'

'You're mighty annoyed at her, for a woman who's not your ex,' Steph observed, seeing his tightly clenched jaw.

'Ex's henchwoman . . . Bridezilla's bridesmaid.'

'Oh, well, that explains things better . . . ' Steph realised she barely knew Jack at all. Of course he had a past, as did she — but she knew nothing about it. Had she gone and put her foot in it? Was he secretly brooding over a lost lover?

Even though she still had no details as to why Jack was so riled by the post-dinner portal to his past, it felt bad to drag it out of him. She opted to try and gloss over it with humour instead.

'What did she do? Victimise the vicar? Hog the honeymoon and become an unwelcome visitor?'

Steph was trying to lighten him up. Okay maybe this wasn't the most sensitive topic to be funny about — but that was one of the perils of Manuel refilling her champagne glass so often. Plus Jack could usually laugh and turn the other cheek.

Clearly not this time.

He turned with a look of thunder, his eyes narrowed and hard, then gave her both barrels unleashed.

'Virginia Johnson gave me the news that I was being jilted then immediately offered her services if I needed cheering up. She was pretty put out that I refused; apparently she's irresistible in her own estimations.

'She and Paula had struck a deal that Virginia could have the leftovers. I figured they deserve each other but I don't think she ever forgave me for not accepting her affections. She likes to worry the old wound, revisit the dumped heir of Glen Muir. End of story. End result — a dinner date ruined by a woman with an acid tongue.'

Steph suddenly wished she could take her size six boot off and shove it in her mouth. Sorry seemed inappropriate and she gave a low whistle. 'Jack, I'm so sorry I made light of it.'

'Don't worry. The woman's a menace but I shouldn't let her get to me. Maybe I need classes in channelling my frustrations better around Virginia?'

Steph watched as Jack shoved his hand through his hair and scuffed his foot in the sand. He looked wonderful, all windswept and spent, post-anger. And a part of her longed to give him the good, hard hug she figured he needed more than anything.

'I'd lie and say she seemed lovely, but I detected the hyena gleam in her eye,' Steph confided. 'You gave her a pretty good roasting though. Top marks.'

'Hyena's an understatement,' Jack elaborated. 'Virginia likes to kick a man when he's down and eat him for breakfast.'

Steph put her hand up to tame her wind-tousled locks. 'Now I can see why you wanted an early exit.'

'And now she's made me spoil our meal.'

Their evening had bombed, that was true, but it wasn't Jack's fault. And at least Steph now knew for certain that it wasn't her presence that had caused it.

'We could adjourn to the Glen Muir bar for a coffee, since ours was rudely interrupted?' she offered.

'Sometimes the moment gets lost,' he replied and began to walk off. Steph followed but within seconds and with a half gasp, half yelp she stumbled and twisted her foot, almost falling into the wiry dune bushes at the side of the pathway.

In seconds Jack was back and holding her in his strong arms. He smelled better than the seashore; his face darker than a highwayman's by moonlight. Her pulse was in her throat and all she could do was stare at those temptingly full lips.

'My boots . . . you were right . . . the path . . . '

'Dangerous.' His breath fanned her cheek as his grip tightened on her waist.

Her heart was hammering at triple speed and the phrase 'feeling flustered' had never held such significance. She was in Jack McGregor's strong embrace and it felt like getting a glimpse of nirvana without preparation.

'I'm sorry she came in,' he mumbled, their lips now so close and tempting it seemed a shame to waste the moment.

'I'm sorry you were jilted. That must've been awful.'

'Ancient history, except in Abercarrick — a man's never allowed to forget.'

Steph seized the initiative to knock the issue on its rusty head. 'I'm not from Abercarrick.'

Jack's eyes were blazing down into hers in the moonlight. 'You haven't sprained your ankle?'

'Just a stumble.'

'Those boots are sexy . . . but just a bit unsuitable for sand.'

Steph faked a pout. 'And since I didn't know where I was coming, I guess we're both to blame.'

Jack righted her then stood back. He'd broken the contact and somehow that was worse than if he'd gone a little crazy. 'Any other flaws in this evening?'

Yes. You didn't kiss me just then, Steph thought.

'Jack, I'm sorry about the wrecked night, but I've had worse, so please, don't get upset about it.'

In the end he said nothing more. He unlocked the car and silently they both got inside.

He reached out his hand and touched her cheek. His touch caused every part of her to ache and yearn and react. It would be so easy, too easy, but she pulled back. She wanted more, but couldn't risk it.

Jack leaned forward, the leather seat squeaking in protest. She could smell his musky cologne and feel the heat of him in the close confines of the car. Worse than that, she could see the look in his eyes — raw pain mixed with raw desire.

But kissing him right now would not be appropriate, not when he was such a tangled mess of emotions. If he kissed her, she needed to be sure it wasn't to settle old scores.

'Steph . . . '

'We must be sensible, Jack.'

He sat back against the leather with a semi groan. She could feel the frustration in the man and while she had huge empathy, she had no words to fit his needs.

'Jack gets it wrong again, huh?' he said wryly.

'No. It's Steph who needs to be

sensible. I'm a passing visitor to Glen Muir and we're working together. Let's keep this in perspective.'

Jack kicked over the ignition, his jaw clenched tight.

'I'm being crazy. Loud and clear.'

She stayed silent for the rest of the journey home.

★　★　★

They drove with their views or further pleasantries on mute. A brooding silence lingered and made them shift awkwardly from time to time to lift it.

'Are you cold?' Jack asked.

Steph shook her head to avoid further exchange.

Jack really wanted to talk properly but for once the words failed him; he resigned himself to a difficult silence.

What would she think of him now? Would she believe him if he told her Virginia had always enjoyed twisting the truth and twisting the knife of revenge for snubbing her?

'Hell hath no fury' really summed their predicament up — but tonight had been unexpected and he hadn't been prepared.

Paula, and by default her accomplice, Virginia, were still thorns in Jack's side and he was weary of it, even with the knowledge that Paula had been the one in the wrong.

Paula had walked out a week before their wedding. At the time, a bout of depression had been his solace and self-protection — and he'd almost lost the job he loved as a result.

Jack shook the memories away; they still inspired anger, and they probably always would.

In the restaurant Steph had looked at him oddly. Then, worse, she'd shown reproach.

And yet before Virginia had dampened things those same eyes had sparkled like agate when she'd laughed and made him feel like some deity of wit and wisdom. She had more feminine wiles than all the women he'd ever met combined.

Jack knew he'd had to muster all the power of self-control at his disposal not to reach right over and kiss her, feel her soft warmth in his arms.

How could one woman fill his senses in so little time? He'd felt her fear and resistance when he'd touched her, and he'd lost his nerve — fool that he was.

'You sure you aren't cold?' he asked again. The silence was now a heavy, suffocating black blanket.

'I'm fine. Let's just get back.'

He felt her beside him in the passenger seat, aware of the smell of her summery perfume and the determined tilt of her chin as she stared ahead.

Her bewitching combination of adversity, challenge and vulnerability had him hooked.

'I'm fine, Jack,' she whispered. 'Are you?'

'I've had better nights.'

Steph's fierce loyalty to Ally and Fraser had him sorely wishing he had her in his own camp. He'd feel twice the man he did if he had Steph at his side.

'I'm sorry, Jack.'

'Virginia may still claim to be Paula's friend but she just wanted to kick off the action and have a pop at me into the bargain. She wanted to cause trouble between us. No doubt it'll be all over the place by tomorrow that I've got a new woman.'

'From what you said,' Steph ventured, 'you've been badly hurt. People can really disappoint but when it happens at the hands of the ones we trust most, it causes a lot of damage.'

Jack watched her sagely. 'You can say that again.'

He could feel her watching him in the darkness. It felt intimate, the two of them talking candidly, alone and personal in their own little private world. He looked over and found watchful eyes that flitted away when he caught them.

'Can we put tonight behind us?' he asked.

'Of course. I went to a great place with a decent man. That's a good night, by my reckoning.'

They were nearing the Glen Muir's wood-lined avenue and the road was dark and desolate, Jack having taken the narrow road back to the hotel's rear.

When Steph unfastened her seatbelt Jack caught her hand. He placed a key in her palm. 'Take this — you can get in the back way safely without anyone seeing.'

He watched her get out of the car and continued to watch until she was inside. Jack restarted the engine and pulled away, 'Softly, softly, Stephanie Baxter,' he murmured. 'But I won't give up now. You've shown me it can be different.'

He'd vowed not to follow his urges. But tonight he knew she was worth the risk. He may toss and turn into the early hours thinking about her, but he still felt tempted by the promise of things to come.

$\star$ $\star$ $\star$

He'd given her an umbrella and ironically the evening had almost been a washout, thanks to an interfering woman out to cause Jack maximum damage. But was it deserved?

Steph knew she had no basis to judge and had only known him a few days — but something told her he was a victim in this. Jack was a good guy and he'd been wronged; she believed him.

Steph pulled off her borrowed dress. Wearing it seemed premature now, since Jack was no more ready for a relationship than she was. As she slowly took off her make-up, the look in her eyes told of the confused thoughts that swirled behind them.

In some ways, she dreaded seeing Jack again. She even wondered if she should have gone out for dinner with him at all. But she couldn't regret it. Prior to coffee, it had been a dream of a night — and that moment when they had almost kissed would not leave her mind. The restaurant would be a private memory she'd cherish like a treasured keepsake.

Clearly Jack's outburst hadn't been his fault — or was she being naïve again, as she'd been with Charlie?

Always thinking the best of him, she'd excused Charlie when he'd left her stranded and solo at surgeons' dinners — yes, he may have had deep problems, but he'd had a sensible and professional job.

Would she have trusted him with her life? Not if there had been a blackjack table nearby or an important game at the racecourse. She'd excused him and believed his covering-up. She truly hadn't realised just how far-reaching his problem was.

Steph studied her reflection as she brushed her teeth before bed. She was just Steph Baxter, a woman who'd had her trust betrayed and her bank account depleted. Her heart had been broken by a man who'd never deserved what she'd given him.

The last thing she needed was love. No; she wasn't looking for a boyfriend.

She was jobless, nearly homeless.

Certainly Jack made her pulse race, but there was nothing that would make her reconsider. Things would have to stay strictly professional with Jack from now on.

It was only as she switched off the bedside lamp that Steph realised she hadn't broached her thoughts on future marketing opportunities for the hotel. Or even the forthcoming fair.

The evening had fallen apart and now she wasn't even sure she wanted to stay around any more. Right now she'd happily pack and go home, were it not for her promises to her friends.

8

Next morning insistent rapping in the door woke Steph at seven. She scrunched her eyes up before grasping her travel alarm clock and got out of bed with a groan. 'Who is it?'

'It's me. Jess.'

Steph pulled her robe around her as she opened the door and saw Jess standing with a tray of domed plates and a steaming coffee pot for one.

'What have I done? Won the lottery?'

'Nope. I need your help sharpish today so I'm buttering you up with a no-holds-barred breakfast. Full Scottish, fresh coffee and juice — the works. Please don't tell me you're a strictly yoghurt girl and I've guessed it wrong.'

Steph yawned and stretched. 'I love a hearty hotel brekkie more than jewels from Bond Street. You're an angel. I really don't deserve you.'

Jess laid the tray on the table by the window. 'So — half an hour in reception? Can you manage to wolf this and shower in time? You're needed.'

'I can do anything when I'm bribed.' Steph pulled up her chair, uncovering her tray's delights. 'Just please don't tell me you're making me practise tossing cabers for tomorrow's show.'

'You'll find out soon,' Jess said, closing the door with a nod.

What was it with the Glen Muir locals and their preferences for mysteries?

★ ★ ★

When Steph reached reception, wearing her hotel uniform and feeling ready for whatever task Jess had in mind, she was in for an unexpected shock.

'Not today, Miss.' Jess took her by the arm and marched her in the direction of Glen Muir's spa.

'What's going on?'

'Boss's orders. You're booked in to be

waxed and polished.'

'You make me sound like an old banger!' Steph laughed.

'I'd never stoop so low. Okay, not waxed — but primped and pampered then. The treatments here are amazing. Consider it an induction and you're getting the works.'

'I've seen the brochure and I've already booked a pedicure for Sunday.'

'Let's just say you're about to get the full monty with bells on, courtesy of Jack McGregor. What did you do — find him a hidden gold mine in the hills of Glen Muir?'

Steph blushed crimson and looked at her feet.

For one she was totally overwhelmed with this morning's 'surprises'. And secondly, if Jess knew the truth of their disastrous night out together it would give the staff gossip for weeks. She wasn't about to go there, and as much as she trusted Jess now, revelations about the night before were not for public consumption.

'So, what're you waiting for, girlie?' Jess cajoled her as Shona came through to the desk and handed Steph a pair of crisp white waffle slippers and the kind of robe you wanted to dive into and never come out of.

Jess waggled her fingers in a wave as Steph followed Shona's lead towards the tranquil haven of Glen Muir's spa rooms and pool.

'Breakfast and now this. Is it my birthday?'

Shona smiled serenely. 'Well, you can't possibly market Glen Muir's full potential as a spa of excellence if you haven't tried us out. I'll see you when you're changed.'

* * *

The morning was a sensual nirvana. Steph, who'd only ever had a manicure in her life as a concession to indulgence, was kneaded and rejuvenated in the nicest possible ways.

After the fairy godmother of all

facials, she had a reflexology treatment followed by some blissful aromatherapy massage that made her feel like heavenly jelly.

Allowed to go and recline in an amazing 'chill room' with low lighting, soothing music, fur throws on its beds and nothing to do but let herself lie back and take it all in, she felt as if she'd gone to heaven.

Steph had never wanted to be rich. In fact, perhaps that was the essential basic difference that should have alerted to her to the issues between her and Charlie. Money and material things only mattered on a basic level — as long as she could pay her rent and have an occasional treat, she was content.

With Charlie his aspirations had always soared ever higher. Hence the gambling drive. He'd loved the thrills of chasing the big win. He'd craved the best suits, the finest holidays, a car that made everyone stop and admire.

Steph stalled her train of thought. She was supposed to be chilling, not reminiscing on life's sore points, but if this was how the rich lived . . . she'd quite fancy indulging in regular spa visits to banish life's strains, even just one a year, if this is how they made you feel.

She nestled back on her day bed and let the music wash over her, calming and soothing.

The letter in her robe pocket crinkled as she moved and made her smile. When she'd emerged from the changing rooms and went to her locker — there had been an envelope awaiting her.

Steph had been written in a bold but neat script. It was a note from Jack.

Last night was a washout and I apologise. It was all my fault. Excuse the duplicity but I wanted to spoil you and knew you wouldn't agree. Please take the morning off and indulge yourself. Shona will look after you. Besides, you need to get up to speed if you're going to be marketing the business, don't you? Go be pampered.

Jack.

Steph wondered if she really could stick to her earlier determination to steer well clear of Jack when he swept her off her feet so ably at every turn.

⋆　⋆　⋆

'And now your lunch is waiting,' Shona said, after presenting Steph with nails that couldn't possibly be attached to her own fingers as they shone in the most perfect shade of pearly pink.

Steph beamed at her in gratitude, wiggling her fingers in front of herself to admire them. 'Do you sideline as a magician?'

'I'm trained to the eyeballs and I've worked in the business of complementary therapies for twelve years.'

'Surely you deserve an OBE.'

Shona grinned, clearly pleased with herself. 'That good, eh?'

'More than you can imagine.'

The light but delicious lunch that awaited her in the tranquil spa bistro, overlooking a small Italianate hotel courtyard garden, was divine, too.

The waitress appeared swiftly to clear away her plate. Steph knew that ordering coffee was probably a no-no after so much 'cleansing' so instead she asked for a herbal tea.

The waitress was a new face, so Steph introduced herself and discovered her name was Kylie. 'Have you been working here long?' Steph asked. She was keen to get to know the staff now and enjoyed meeting so many people.

'I'm temping here before university. I'm off soon to study music in Glasgow.'

'Congratulations. What instrument?' Steph asked intrigued.

'What don't I play? My dad calls me a one-woman band. Saxaphone, Spanish guitar, piano, violin. Of course my favourite is the drums.'

Steph was both impressed and surprised. 'You don't look like a drummer.'

'I've been playing drums since I was six. I'm in a band; in fact that's my only major regret about leaving Glen Muir for Glasgow. I won't be able to keep playing in the Tartan Samba Band.'

Steph grinned at the revelation. 'Tartan Samba Band? I'm fascinated.'

'We don kilts and drum in samba style — trumpets and percussion, too — and loud! It gets everyone dancing and we all love it. We go around fairs and fêtes doing our thing. It's addictive, full of energy and the best mood-lifter in the world.'

'I'd love to hear you sometime. Do you play at the hotel?'

'No. It's not exactly in keeping with Glen Muir's five-star status. Sometimes I play piano in the bar here for extra cash.'

Kylie pushed her hand into her apron pocket and brought out a card. 'Here. This is our website. Maybe you can catch the band — there's a dates listing on the site.'

Steph tucked the card in her robe pocket and made a mental note to look it up as Kylie bid her goodbye and

Steph finished her tea. By her reckoning, she had an hour — and then she'd be meeting Jack to go and visit Ally.

'All play and no work, eh?' Steph muttered to herself, and with the smile of contentment, went to get changed.

★ ★ ★

When she met Jack again his humour had returned to the easy, bright manner she'd grown to enjoy. Fortunately they'd both apparently resolved to draw a line under the night before.

'You shouldn't have, you know,' she said when she reached him in reception. He was wearing deep navy jeans and a striped golf shirt that did everything right for his frame.

'Shouldn't have what?' his eyes darkened. 'About last night — I'm sorry. Didn't you get the note?'

'Yes, I did, and it was very kind and thoughtful. But last night wasn't your fault and you really didn't have anything to apologise for in the first place. I mean the spa treatments, the full works pampering; it must have cost an arm and a leg.'

'I like to know I'm looking after the people that matter.'

'There's looking after, and then there's treating me like a princess. I don't deserve it, Jack . . . if you'll let me repay you . . . ?'

Jack's expression became almost annoyed. 'Call it an employees' perk. You enjoyed it? That's the point.'

'Very much. I hadn't even realised what hot stones were. And fragrant mud and a good pummel can turn your whole body to velvet. No wonder people go in for these spas in a big way.'

Jack's eyes darkened and Steph quickly realised perhaps she shouldn't have been so free and easy with her descriptions of how her body felt after hours of luxurious treatments, but it had been wonderful; she felt so relaxed and cherished — and that was all down to him.

She blushed. Aware she'd said too much.

'Ah, so now you have acquired a taste for the high life.'

'And now I'm jobless, the closest I'll get to hot stones is a shingle beach during a heatwave without flip-flops.'

Jack stuffed his hands in jeans pockets. 'I don't think you'll be unemployed for long. Call it a hunch.'

'Thank you anyway. Your kindness was breathtaking.'

'You're welcome.' His smile dazzled her as much as the treatments had done. So much power and energy in that combination of wide lips and strong, white teeth, it made her want to do nothing but just want to sit and bask in the warmth.

'C'mon, Prima Donna. No more primping for you — it's time to go,' he teased her.

The next hour and a quarter's journey to the hospital passed in friendly, neutral exchange with Jack. The awkwardness of the night before had gone. He told her about life since the castle had been renovated into a hotel, from refurbishments to setting up a hotel from scratch.

She noted how animated it made him — he clearly loved Glen Muir, and she loved it when his eyes crinkled when he smiled.

'There are plenty of things that you grow to love when you take the plunge. I never thought I'd ever be an hotelier but I enjoy it. I like that it brings new people to my home and they enjoy it so much — plus it helps fund the estate.'

He caught her gaze and his look stirred her deeply. He paused before he continued, 'Haven't you ever been bowled over by something you'd dismissed out of turn?' His eyes flashed her a challenge. 'Living spontaneously can be a good thing,' he added, glancing at her as he drove.

'Spontaneity can bring danger and risk, though,' she replied honestly, taking control of herself. 'I don't take many risks and I guess that's why the redundancy thing rocked me. I like regularity, routine and due warning.'

'A preference for control?'

'Absolutely.'

After Charlie — and the loss of control he'd wreaked on her life — it was her constant.

Jack watched her, his eyes deep and dark. 'Maybe I'll make it my mission to tempt you into some new adventures? Clay pigeon shooting, golf . . . maybe another dinner since I bodged up last night so badly?'

'Jack, let's keep things light. You haven't been set up by Fraser and Ally to bring me here, have you?'

'Set up — how d'you mean?' He threw a searching glance.

'Ally treats me like the longest-serving member of Spinsters Anonymous.' She shot her eyes skyward. 'It wouldn't surprise me if they'd set us up. She's well-meaning, but still misguided. I'm not looking for love or relationships.'

She fiddled with her watch strap, avoiding his gaze, then remembered Charlie had given her that watch. She wondered if it had been his way of buying her off to placate his conscience.

'Actually, Fraser's exact words to me

were, 'Jack, I need you. I'm trusting you with my wife's best friend. Look after her and drive carefully'.' A loaded silence hung in the air; heavy with inference and potency.

She'd been trying to state things clearly, but had she now gone and overstepped the mark? She'd tried hard to work out how to play her cards with Jack and now she felt like an idiot for suggesting he was driven by dating.

Jack sighed. 'In answer to your question — no, Fraser didn't set you up. I offered to bring you.'

She narrowed her eyes into the sunshine and held her hand up to shield them and saw the hospital coming into view. It was a large high building with sprawling wings.

'We're here. Ally's going to be so glad to see you.'

'It looks enormous. I hope we find her.'

'I know my way. Trust me, I'm a doctor.' He grinned. 'I'm better at navigating than dinner dates.'

Jack parked and they got out of the car. His mouth was set when he spoke next. 'Why do you question my motives, Steph?'

She watched transfixed as he ran his tongue over his lips and his eyes narrowed. With a shake of his dark head, he walked around the car and placed a gentle hand on her shoulder. It sent pleasurable shockwaves through her body, even as the alarm bells went off in her head.

'I wanted to come here. I have some business later and it was a case of killing two birds with one stone,' Jack informed her gravely. 'Come on, let's go and see your friend.'

Steph followed his lead to the hospital entrance, preoccupied by her realisation that having her body space invaded by him was always something she wasn't ready for — and yet she craved it somehow.

What was it with that man that he could manage to reduce her to a quivering wreck so regularly? It really had been too long since Charlie if she was about to fall at Jack's feet the moment he came anywhere near her — making her forget that Jack McGregor was supposed to stay firmly off limits in her rulebook.

9

Ally looked inside the two bags of goodies Steph had brought with her and declared, 'You've bought half of Niven and Hazel's magazine racks here.'

Steph and Jack's warm greetings had been accepted as she clamoured to see what she'd been brought in the way of supplies. Steph almost shuddered at the thought of the contraband Fraser had sent to his wife . . . crackers, peanut butter and Wensleydale cheese. Apparently since pregnancy, Ally's cravings had taken a turn for the strange.

'This place is like prison. How much daytime TV can a girl stand?' Ally shoved her finger into the jar and greedily scooped out a blob of the gooey butter. Steph tried not to look.

'Then you'll be really pleased that I've brought you these,' Steph said, presenting her with yet another bag. 'Knitting magazines, wool and needles. I thought you could make something nice for the baby and it'll help pass the time, too. Jess supplied the kit.'

'Knitting? I haven't knitted since I was in my teens. I suppose I may as well give it a try, since the outside world has locked me up and thrown away the key.'

'Now, Ally, it's all for the sake of the little one on board.'

'I know,' Ally whispered as if rumbled. 'I just like to complain because you know I can't stand staying in one place — especially one with no gossip.'

'Then I'll instruct Jess to write you a full debrief of all Glen Muir's tittle-tattle tales,' Jack put in, and they laughed in unison.

Steph saw Jack watching as she hugged Ally, and she cast him a glance that told him he might want to make his escape.

'I'll go and find some coffees and attend to a few things I need to do — is there anything else you need, Ally?'

He raised an eyebrow and leaned casually on the door frame. He looked great in his soft leather jacket, and Steph had definitely seen a clutch of nurses admiring him while they were wandering through the wards looking for Ally.

She didn't think he'd even noticed them watching, which only increased his appeal. There were so many traits to recommend him; the little gestures that she was starting to recognise as typically Jack, from the way he tilted his head when he watched her to the roguish grin he employed, with killer results.

'Don't think so,' Ally replied. 'No — on second thoughts . . . could you bring some liquorice?'

'Surely you don't need more strange food?' Steph laughed.

'It's not for me. One of the nurses is mad for it and she's been trading me home-made chocolate cake.' Ally grinned like the naughtiest schoolgirl in the school.

'A girl's gotta do what she can to get by.'

Jack's face was a picture as he left. 'I'll see what I can do.'

'How are you feeling? Fraser's been keeping me updated.'

'Much better. Just annoyed at being stuck in here.'

'But you need the rest, Ally.' Steph saw that in spite of the recovered appetite, her friend's complexion was pale and rather more gaunt than she would have liked.

'But this place is boring, and there's so much at the hotel I should be dealing with,' Ally protested. 'Beam me back to Glen Muir, Scotty.'

'Tell me what needs to be done,' Steph demanded as she arranged fruit artistically in a bowl.

'The Highland fair for starters.'

'Under control. I'm in charge.'

'You?'

'Yes — with Jack's help, of course, but I'm really enjoying being involved. So that's one less worry. Anything else?'

'We need to order chairs for the new conference room for the painting course starting at the end of next week. There's a file for it, but getting the chairs was my one outstanding task. Then you need to call Archie Flynn, the artist, and tell him he'll need to run it solo. He'll instruct you with his needs for refreshment orders and so on.'

'Consider it done,' Steph declared. 'I think I'll be good at chair testing and I'm glad to get the chance to prove myself.' Steph laughed. 'How long will you be in here?'

'Until baby comes — that's about forty days too many by my reckoning.' Ally rubbed at her bump as if it were a genie's lamp. 'So what've you been up to?'

'Just settling in, growing to love the hotel, getting to know everyone, the usual,' Steph said. 'We've been really busy what with one thing and another.'

And let's not even talk about the Jack McGregor effect, she thought to herself.

'What do you think of the dashing doc, then?' Ally shot her a wicked glance. 'And before you deny it, give me some credit for brains. He's great, isn't he?'

Steph glared. 'What are you like? Keep your voice down, he might come back. And no — you've been reading too many paperbacks — I've been too busy to notice anyone or anything.'

This was all Steph needed — Ally on her case, cajoling, probing, seeing things that weren't even there. Had the way they shared glances given her away?

'Jack's a good-looking guy, you'd be nuts not to notice him. But just rein it in a bit because he's off the menu. It would be one very bad move you don't need.'

Steph looked at her incredulously, unable to think of the right words. She'd expected match-making and encouragements; not reverse psychology.

Eventually she said, 'For starters there is absolutely nothing between us, nor am I remotely interested. In fact, right now I'm reminding myself exactly why I bothered to travel hundreds of miles to see you when all you ever do is lecture me.'

Ally paused, biting back the words she'd been about to say. 'Sorry — it's just a warning between friends. I love Jack to bits but he has issues from his past that would make it a very unwise move for both of you, that's all. It was meant for the best. It'd be dangerous waters for you both. His brother really hurt him, Steph, and I don't think he's over it all.'

'His brother. Hamish, right?'

'Hamish let us down badly,' Ally began. 'He'd initially been the one to enter discussions on the partnership running the hotel, but then he disappeared, left us in the lurch. Fortunately Jack stepped in but there was a huge fight. Hamish McGregor is a name that shouldn't be mentioned around Glen Muir. No one even knows where exactly in Sydney he's gone, except

Jack, and he won't talk about it to anyone. People ask me about Hamish all the time.'

Steph seized the chance to do some reverse psychology of her own. 'So I'm not good enough for your precious business partner, then?'

Ally groaned, 'No, Steph, I just mean he's not ready for a relationship yet. He's been through a lot and he needs time to heal. Girlfriends and romantic involvement are firmly out of bounds for Jack McGregor.'

'Does he know you take such a keen interest in his private life?' Steph quizzed, losing patience with Ally's know-it-all air.

'Jack needs me to look out for him.' Ally pushed herself higher up in bed. If she'd thought the trip to the hospital was going to be solely for the intention of lectures and warnings she'd have stayed at home and watched daytime television instead, Steph thought in irritation. 'You're a great girl and you deserve to meet someone great, after

Charlie,' Ally went on.

Steph stiffened visibly at this ill-considered comment. She stared at her boots unable to conjure a suitable comeback.

'Steph — what a stupid thing to say!' Ally responded. 'I'm sorry. I think the hormones are affecting my brain.'

'You're right,' Steph regarded her friend levelly. 'And not about the hormones. Charlie Hughes is my past and I need to move on now. Coming to Glen Muir has made me realise I'm still letting it all haunt me, I suppose because he damaged my trust and crushed my self-esteem, made me wonder who I can trust — question if I can even trust my own judgement.'

She moved away to rearrange the flowers in their vase to avoid further probing. 'Jack let Hilary go and he's asked me to help with marketing ideas, that's all. I might be able to help.'

Ally rubbed her bump and grinned. 'That's a great idea. He's picked the right woman for the job. I told you

Jack's got a good head on his shoulders.'

Steph had thought it all through and she knew some of her ideas would work without reservation. The most crucial one was the one she needed to broach with Ally now.

'I'd like to invest my redundancy money in advertising to generate bookings for Glen Muir. I have ideas about other changes that I'll run past Jack but first I wanted your consent. Will you let me help out with a promotional budget? I want to help however I can.'

Ally's eyes brimmed with tears and she quickly put her hand to her lips.

'Hey, don't get upset — it's not good for you or the baby.' Steph rushed to Ally's side.

'You'd do that for us?' Ally said, her voice catching.

Steph gave her a steady look. 'Who else do I trust above all others? Apart from my mum and dad you're the next best thing to family. Plus my parents have given me a nest egg from their wool shop business to help me secure a new flat. It's just sitting in the bank gaining interest and I'd rather use it to help you. What else are friends for?'

The women hugged. 'Glen Muir is going to be booked to the rafters soon.' Steph rubbed Ally's back and then both of them smiled at each other.

Jack stood in the doorway, looking uncomfortable and bearing two cups of cappuccino and a vast box of liquorice Allsorts. 'Want me to scarper for a bit?'

He really looked appealing when he was feeling awkward.

'Come on in and tell me how tricks are with you,' Ally instructed and gave Steph's hand a squeeze.

Jack grinned. 'I'm good. Did I tell you I'm coaching a young woman to run a Highland fair? She's good, too — she might be a keeper for hotel work in the future.' Jack winked. 'If she stops the back chat, that is.'

'Tell me all about her, Jack. I'm all ears,' said Ally rubbing her bump with vigour. 'Cheer me up with stories of this new apprentice. Though I have a hunch I may have met her already.'

★ ★ ★

When they left the hospital after visiting time, Jack still had some business errands to run. The evening light was dimming when he pulled up outside a stately-looking Georgian house.

It was the kind of abode often featured in dolls' house designs; large, imposing and picturesque. Its location, in a wealthy street on the outskirts of town, told this was the home of some-one who'd worked hard and reaped the rewards.

'I just need to drop off some papers, you don't mind waiting for a few minutes, do you?'

He watched Steph sitting in the passenger seat of his car. She looked adorable, casually dressed in jeans and a light jacket. Her smile lit him up inside and he surmised she probably

150

didn't even have a clue how she caused something new and exciting to kindle within him.

Jack smiled, then walked up the path to the large, glossy black door. He was admitted by a bespectacled gentleman amid a flurry of dogs barking.

'Mr McFadyen. Thanks for seeing me at such short notice.'

'Legal matters wait for no man. It's a pleasure, Jack. Terrible business with your father, but we were right to be prepared in the first place.'

'I've done all you requested.'

Soon enough the papers were dealt with, instructions left, and Jack headed down the crunchy gravel path back to the car.

Part of him was relieved that power of attorney had finally been actioned, but he was saddened too. It marked another step in the diminishment of his father.

Even though he'd specified as and when Jack should take full control, it was still hard to accept. Lately he'd realised that point had come. Jack knew he had to be proactive in this — and his father had been thorough in his preparations while he'd still had lucid moments.

But it was the the letter to Hamish that had really caused Jack's heart to clench.

'That's sorted . . . are you okay?' he asked when he climbed back in behind the wheel again.

'Yes. Finished your business?'

'For now.' He restarted the engine.

Formalities done for now. Responsibilities for him; huge responsibilities. And an inevitable backlash down the line.

★   ★   ★

Steph's phone rang just as she and Jack were pulling up Glen Muir's long avenue approach road, beneath its leafy oak trees in the dawning darkness. She answered it swiftly even though she didn't recognise the number.

'Hello. Is that Ms Stephanie Baxter?' asked an unfamiliar but particularly burry male voice.

'It is. Who's calling?'

'Angus McArthur. Jess Cameron gave me your number; I'm the band leader for the Glen Muir Pipe Band. It's bad news I'm afraid. We're on the Isle of Skye and our transport's conked out. The relay company won't tow us all home. There's no way we'll make tomorrow's fair.'

Steph inwardly groaned. But then again, for Angus McArthur getting to the fair was the least of his worries and he was being good enough to tell her. But if these guys were 'The Glen Muir band', that made them their star turn.

Steph looked at Jack who was still driving and tried to disguise her whirling state of mind.

'I'm sorry to hear that, Mr McArthur.' She watched as Jack's brows quirked in puzzlement but she shook her head. 'Don't worry. Just get yourselves home safe and sound.'

'We've booked into a guest house but I wanted to give you fair warning. I'm sorry to let you down.'

'That's okay. I hope you manage to get back on the road soon.' Steph gently clicked shut her phone and sighed.

'Angus equals band, equals . . . ?' asked Jack, perceptive as ever. His dark, thick hair gleamed from the lights from the dashboard in the car's dim interior, making her long to touch it, just to see if it felt as good as it looked. But now — mid band crisis — wasn't the moment; was her brain trying to escape in such sensory details?

'Angus is stuck on Skye,' she said. 'So we've no band for tomorrow.' She bit her lip. 'It's not the man's fault.'

'Shame, but can't be helped.'

She hadn't expected him to be quite as matter-of-fact about it. Suddenly the stark contrast between Jack and Charlie hit her with full force.

Charlie would have been going crazy — when things in his life went awry, so did he, which was probably why Steph truly appreciated that Jack McGregor stayed calm and in control whatever the crisis. Even with Virginia there had never been any question that he'd been in full control of his faculties. How a man ought to be, in fact.

'Weren't they supposed to be doing a parade on the green?' Steph mused. 'And there was going to be Highland dancing with them as accompaniment? The file says they were judging things too . . . ' Steph added anxiously.

'Miracles aren't my forte. Sometimes things happen and you just have to accept them,' Jack answered. 'It's okay — just use a CD on the tannoy for the dancing and we'll just have to pass on the parade thing.'

'But I don't want the event to be lacking, Jack. It matters. Call it personal pride, call it redundancy stubbornness — I want tomorrow to be amazing.'

'Steph. You're only human. Things crop up.'

As Jack reached the hotel Steph firmed her conviction to do something.

She may be an interim aide on this project but she wasn't ready to let it slip; Ally was relying on her. So far she'd felt like a cheat with little to do — now was her time to pull out all the stops.

She got out of the car as soon as it stopped and turned to run towards the hotel.

'Hey! Aren't you going to say goodbye? Thank me for being the most riveting, handsome driving companion you've ever had? Congratulate me on finding liquorice to placate your crazy best friend?' Jack was feigning hurt but with his tongue clearly in his cheek. He was so handsome it made her toes curl.

'Sorry, Jack, you know you're the best, but I've got to dash; duty calls and all that . . . '

She had a hunch she just knew could be the solution she needed — with the help of a certain drummer/saxophonist who'd been looking for a big break.

The only answer that eluded her was why it was so very important to her to prove herself to Jack McGregor.

She wanted to repay him, to prove herself as proficient — and maybe she'd also quite like him to be bowled over by what she knew she was capable of.

The pre-redundancy-jaded Steph was back and she was raring to get to it.

10

The next morning dawned bright and fresh, complete with a cloudless sky and birds chirping tunefully in the trees outside Steph's room. It heralded the day ahead; the Glen Muir Highland Fair was upon her.

When she'd opened her eyes in bed, the first thing that had entered Steph's waking mind was the look on Jack's face as she'd dashed from the car.

She knew she'd have to explain later that there was method in her madness, and the phone call she'd had with Kylie had yielded results. After making a good case for her Tartan Samba Band's involvement next day, she'd received a confirmation call-back that the band were ready to oblige.

Kylie had been a lifesaver — and in truth Steph couldn't wait to witness their efforts. She'd gone to bed grateful for the mine of local, willing talent available in Glen Muir.

Steph rose at six, showered and dressed quickly, then breakfasted simply on crackers and coffee in her room.

By the time she got down to greet the grounds crew outside, butterflies were whirling inside her as adrenaline surged, but soon she was hefting tables and altering layouts as the crew systematically set up every marquee to match Steph's detailed ground plans.

It was going to be a busy day; greeting exhibitors, checking arrangements and trouble-shooting problems. All she had to concentrate on now was doing it.

★　★　★

The fair opened at eleven and by noon visitors were queuing at the gates and milling around stalls and the event ring and staging area, where a series of displays had been scheduled.

There was plenty to do, and the

sights and smells had Steph itching to lay down her walkie talkie and clipboard for a while and just visit the exhibits herself. She vowed to make time later.

A craft tent was selling everything from paintings to hand-made iron garden sculpture, wooden bowls and rugs.

The Chef's Corner was Fraser's domain; complete with a display kitchen for cooking demos, and the opportunity for sampling tasters from a farmer's market-styled farm shop.

Visitors were already filling shopping bags when Steph looked inside on one of her frequent tours around the fair.

Outside of the tented area, proud pet owners displayed dogs' agility and on a staged area Highland dancers were doing their stuff. A dimmed complementary therapies tent attracted attendees keen for treatments and a kiddie's spiegeltent featured storytelling, puppetry and crafts.

It was there that Steph bumped into Jess, who was in charge of the children's schedule and was currently staffing the treasure hunt game stall with her partner Gordon.

'Show me these kids of yours, I can't wait to meet them,' Steph said, looking around her at the gaggle of children and trying to pick them out.

'My rascals are over there.' Jess pointed out a dark-haired boy and a girl with shoulder-length French-braided hair and a yellow sundress with a border of bright daisies. 'One's craft mad, the other just wants to play football and be a superhero.'

Steph laughed. 'At least they know what they like.'

'You should've seen the fuss we had prising Blair out of his Spiderman suit — he wears it everywhere. I insisted the hero antics and web skills had to stay at home today. Kids, eh?'

'As busy as their mum,' quipped Steph. 'Everything okay?'

'More than okay, it's brilliant. The Samba band are amazing. Suddenly Blair wants to play in a drum band and wear a kilt when he's grown up.'

'They were late-notice lifesavers,' Steph explained. 'I think they're adding a fresh edge. It's going well . . . '

A crackly voice, known to her well now as Murdo Stephenson, head groundsman, came over her walkie talkie.

'Ooops, spoke too soon,' Steph said.

'You're wanted on the gate, Steph,' he said in his thick Scots brogue. 'Some details I need checking. In your own time.'

'Roger that,' Steph said, developing her walkie-talkie skills and giggling along with Jess like a schoolgirl. 'Want me to bring a bacon roll with me?'

'Now you're just sweet-talkin' me, lassie,' Murdo answered.

'Just keeping important staff on side. Red sauce or brown?'

'Brown. And the bacon done crispy.'

With a smile she went off through the crowds. She might even buy a second Murdo special for herself.

★ ★ ★

While Steph waited for her rolls to be made just the way Murdo liked, she spied a stall that caught her immediate attention; it was a small but corporately-styled marquee, bearing the logo of the soap-maker she'd seen displayed in the spa, Simply Scottish Soaps.

Her interest was immediately piqued since she'd tried the samples and already felt that Jack should be making links with this business for mutual gain.

Fighting the urge to let her attention stray to their fabulous gift baskets, she introduced herself to the woman behind the stall.

'I'm Maura Gilmore. I make the soaps by hand myself. It's always been my dream to start my own business, so I went on a course and started with soaps — just a small range of three scents — and things have grown well. It's all essential oils and natural ingredients with no nasty additives or preservatives. Our emphasis is on local and natural but luxurious.'

'I'm a fan already. Shona in the Glen

Muir spa gave me samples,' Steph confided. 'How long have you been trading?'

'Four years now but internet business is already strong. We'll need bigger premises or more outlets soon because our shop is a tiny roadside log cabin. We're fast running out of space but that's what happens when you become successful!'

'Could I drop by and see you sometime?' Steph asked.

Maura gave her a card. 'Feel free — any time.'

'I want to buy more,' Steph confided as she heard the woman on the snack stand call out that her order was ready. 'And I'd like to discuss an idea I have about expanding links with Glen Muir. I'll see you soon.'

'I'll look forward to it,' Maura beamed, then turned back to a customer who had her arms filled with her fragrant wares.

Steph went off for Murdo's roll before he started making walkie-talkie demands again.

A tall assured-looking man was striding towards her with a devilish glint in his eye — and this time it wasn't Jack McGregor.

Disappointingly, Steph had only caught the briefest glimpses of Glen Muir's owner during her morning's activities. He'd looked handsome and hands-on in jeans and a Glen Muir-branded polo shirt. She'd hoped he'd stop by and talk but he'd been busy and in high demand.

If truth be told, Steph knew deep down she was starting to get withdrawal symptoms, but she figured that for most of the day, she and Jack would be ships that would pass without banter, so she should put it from her mind and get on.

'Hi there,' the man said as he approached. He raised a brow in a definite smoulder.

Steph racked her brains; should she know him? This man oozed ready confidence as he neared, but Steph kept walking resolutely towards the gate-house.

He wore a chef's white short-sleeved jacket and chequered trousers; he looked like Tuscan chef meets romance novel model. His skin spoke of a hot climate habit and his teeth bore a Hollywood gleam.

'Hello. Leaving so soon?' His swagger told her he knew his looks could draw attention too. 'Naughty girl. Snacking on hot rolls when you could be tasting honey-drizzled figs or chocolate torte in my tent,' he said as she passed by, then added, 'Aren't you going to say hello and tell me who you are?'

'Sorry — busy — can't stop or the boss will berate me.'

'And you are?'

'Steph. Backroom runner at Glen Muir.' On cue her walkie talkie burst into life, but the reception was so bad she couldn't hear what request was being made. She imagined it was Murdo hastening her arrival.

The man watched her with a wry,

open smile on his face. 'Come see me later? I'm Greg, Fraser's special guest, and producing something tasty is my forte. Of course, I don't like to blow my own trumpet, but I'll make you something special to impress you.'

Talk about full on! 'No time for cooking demos for me. I'm working,' Steph said briskly. The delicious bacon rolls in her grasp were already making her stomach rumble and now all this talk of food was making her realise she'd done a lot of hard work on an empty stomach.

His brow quirked into an expression designed to change her mind. 'Why not come and have fun with me later, huh?'

Steph supposed there'd be a lot of women who'd be weakening at the knees for such an invite. She stayed firm.

'They say doing a job well is its own reward. Must dash; I'm delivering food to the crew.'

'Who are you anyway, 'Backroom Steph'?'

The man reached out and righted her

name badge that had twisted on her polo shirt. The open contact made her jump and their eyes met. He clearly wooed women as if tackling an assault course in an armoured tank at full throttle.

'Visit me later, Steph Baxter. I could do with something appetising to look at.'

'You're certainly forward, aren't you?' Steph answered.

'If you don't ask, you don't get.' He winked as he watched her walk away.

This guy didn't just know his own attractions; he trumpeted them across the county. As Steph ruminated on the exchange she snorted. Greg-Flirty-Chef wouldn't be drawing her in anytime soon. Especially when the only tryst she wanted to attend was a private one with the elusive Jack McGregor.

★   ★   ★

'Where's Murdo? He told me he was ravenous.'

When Steph reached the gatehouse marquee she realised she'd been duped.

Jack, sitting alone behind the main desk, patted the chair beside him. Immediately her heart did triple salcos of secret delight. His hair was deliciously tousled, falling casually across his forehead.

'You entering for some Guiness Book of Records accolade in event running?' he teased her.

'Just keeping law and order in the manner Ally would want.'

'Then sit down. Ally isn't here and I'm the boss now. I've watched you running around like a crazy person all morning and decided it was time to intervene.'

'And Murdo?' Steph asked, holding his prized hot roll aloft.

'Ah, deceptive but necessary. I'll take that.' Jack swiftly took the roll and sank his white teeth into it, causing a puff of flour. He grinned, lips powdery white. 'Unbeatable.'

Steph took the seat and copied him.

'I've just been chatted up by some guy who thinks he's God's gift to woman-kind. He offered to cook just for me.' She rolled her eyes for effect.

Jack quickly looked wary. 'Want me to put him in his place good and proper?'

'Given a choice between a bacon roll with you and fine dining with him, I pick the takeaway van.'

Jack grinned broadly and poured her a coffee from his flask. 'Ah, you like me — I knew you were a woman of good taste.'

'Counting your chickens?'

'So, this scurrilous rogue who was chatting you up. Do I have to challenge him to a tossing-the-caber contest?'

'I wasn't so struck on him and I think he's more used to tossing salad than cabers.'

Jack grinned. 'Pleased to hear I'm superior in something. I guess you just can't resist my charm, courtesy and honest upstanding decency.'

'Says the man who got Murdo to

pretend he needed me just to hijack his snack?'

'That's about the size of it. But now you can play hookie with me and enjoy a late brunch and the gentle repartee of the cleverest doctor in Glen Muir.'

'Luckily, I'm hungry and I won't argue,' said Steph. But inside she was very, very glad she'd been fooled, because lately she was utterly addicted to this flirty banter and close contact with Jack McGregor.

'Jack,' she asked while her nerve was still buoyant, 'Can I quickly bend your ear about the spa? I've just been speaking to an amazing woman who makes natural handmade soaps and I know she'd be interested in making links with the hotel — especially the spa.

'Plus there's something worrying me — your spa's run on a tight, limited schedule and Shona's about to go on maternity leave. Have you and Ally and Fraser considered any of this?'

Jack rubbed his jaw. 'So much for

getting time alone. You're starting to obsess about my business, Steph Baxter.'

'Then listen up because there are some suggestions I want to make.' Steph pushed her advantage home.

* * *

'First-aider needed urgently at the play park. Fallen child requires attention.'

When Jack's eyes met hers over his coffee cup the seriousness was in sharp contrast to their earlier banter. 'Let's go,' he said throwing their brunch debris in the bin as he ran.

Steph's heart was pounding fast in her chest as they ran, ducking around gaggles of visitors to get there as fast as possible. Jack reached out to take her hand as the play park came into view, tugging her along in synch with his fast strides.

They reached the park in minutes and found a group gathered around a small, prone figure who was lying on the grass. The sight gave Steph the urge to cry but she knew she had to keep calm and a clear head; panic would not be helpful.

Steph's fear peaked as she recognised the vivid yellow, daisy-bordered dress of Jess's daughter, Lisa.

As she lay on the ground she was making worrying, racking sounds, gasping for breath. Each raspy effort sounded painful and provided little relief for the child. Lisa clearly wanted to cry and call for her mummy but was too affected to do so. Her disorientation was painful to watch.

'She's winded,' said Jack decisively. 'Clear the way. Give us room for treatment here.' The crowd dispersed a little and Murdo went into immediate security-cordoning mode.

'What happened?' Jack asked, diving straight into the incident and gently lifting Lisa to a sitting position. Her body was limp and her face was pale. Jack tenderly brushed back her hair and crooned encouragingly to the child to let her know she would be okay.

Jess was being held back by a worried, wan Gordon. A first aider arrived just then, but allowed Jack to take the lead.

'She fell flat on her back from the top of the climbing frame,' Gordon explained.

'Winded,' said Jack. 'All the oxygen expelled from her body in one hard thud.'

'She got up fine at first but then collapsed again,' said Gordon. 'One minute we were watching her climbing the rope frame, the next she was down. Her foot must've slipped.'

The first-aider added, 'Luckily the play area is built on soft material. It would've been a harder blow if it was Tarmac, given that it was a fall to her back.'

'She can't breathe! Do something!' Jess cried, clearly fraught with panic; mother's protective instincts in over-drive.

Steph went to Jess's side to offer a comforting hug. All the time she observed Jack taking immediate control of this situation, in a calm and professional manner; he was decisive and impressive in the extreme.

'I know it's frightening, Lisa,' Jack murmured softly. 'But you're just winded. Take your time to get a good supply of oxygen going again, just breathe slowly, normally . . . '

Still the tiny figure was labouring over each breath, but slowly her breaths became deeper, her lungs recovering.

'Just let her recover in her own time.' Jack summoned a tearful and shaking Jess to her daughter's side. He squeezed her arm as she thanked him. 'Don't mention it. It's frightening but she'll be fine. Just give her lots of hugs.'

The crisis had been averted, thanks the presence of a skilled doctor with a calm, clear head.

★   ★   ★

There was a crowd of people around the hero of the day and Jess was hugging her daughter and thanking Jack simultaneously. Steph took her cue to disappear discreetly. She had a feeling that those involved would benefit from something to lift away the shadow of crisis — and some space.

Ducking into the kids' tent Steph quickly found the man she needed, surrounded by a hundred vividly coloured balloons. Every animal that could have been made from a balloon, had been. He'd clearly had a busy, dexterity-testing day, twisting rubber to amuse the little ones.

'Can you do me a favour?' Steph asked with her widest smile. 'Could you make me a couple of balloons for a family that have just had a fright? Ideally one with lots of pink, and one to do with Spiderman?'

The balloon maker threw her a wink. 'I like a challenge.'

'Ready in ten minutes?'

'A deadline, too. I'll give it my best shot.'

Steph grinned her thanks then shot

176

off to the tent next door. During set-up she'd spied an exhibitor that she intended to see and she may just be able to come up with a useful addition to Glen Muir's marketing push too.

She swiftly located the local wedding photographer, Malcolm Dundas, at his allotted stand.

Ten minutes later they'd struck a deal. She'd secured what she wanted and had been gratified that he'd been so enthusiastic about her proposal.

Steph returned to Jess's family — now more recovered — her mission complete, and handed over the balloons to Lisa and Blair with a flourish.

'Oh look,' gasped Jess. 'Look what Steph's gone and got you, Lisa! Isn't it wonderful?' The little girl's face showed immediate pleasure, as if the playground incident was a distant memory when faced with a huge flower made up of pink, lilac and yellow balloons. The girl beamed her radiant delight.

'It's a giant magic flower, for being so brave. Blair has one too — Spiderman

— the balloon-maker drew a great Spidey on it!'

Both children were delighted with their impromptu gifts and Steph handed Jess the envelope from the photographer.

'A gift from me. You had a shock and I wanted to do something you'd like. This guy is the best local photographer — it's a voucher so you and your family can get a portrait done in the grounds of the hotel. He has a friend who does hair and make-up too. I thought you deserved a treat and I like to look after my best friends.'

Jess threw her arms around Steph's shoulders. 'You remembered my wish about the wedding pic! Oh, Steph, that's wonderful — thank you!'

'There is a condition,' Steph added. 'I have another motive. If you don't mind, I'd like to use the photos for promoting the hotel as a wedding venue. We need publicity photographs for an ad and a brochure. Your photo-shoot would be part of it.'

'Of course I don't mind. I'd be delighted. And I'll book it as soon as I can.' Jess had tears in her eyes when she pulled back.

'All's well that ends well, right?'

'Right,' Jess agreed, then hugged her again.

11

Everyone at the fair was talking about Jack and his hero status. Fortunately the incident involving Lisa had been a minor mishap. But Jack's part in events was being widely appreciated. However, in tune with his usual self-deprecating style, he'd vanished and was nowhere to be seen.

Steph went to seek out Fraser in the chef's tent. He'd been doing a cookery demo and had missed out on all the fuss. She was explaining what had happened when Greg-Flirty-Chef from earlier appeared at her elbow. He smiled his debonair smile and looked as if he was ready for a second round of charm offensive.

Steph carried on with her hero tale about Jack's medical moment and Greg listened in. Finally Fraser made introductions.

'Have you met Greg Fitzgerald yet?'

Suddenly a light bulb illuminated Steph's earlier puzzle. '*The* Greg Fitzgerald?' Steph said, embarrassed now that she hadn't recognised him. 'London's celeb chef of the moment?'

'The very same,' Greg replied smoothly.

The man was the star of his own Saturday morning cookery programme, no less. How could she not have realised, when his books were in supermarkets and his products were advertised on TV? Steph blamed the dark designer stubble he was sporting.

'I'd no idea we we had such an important cooking star here. Why didn't you tell me earlier, Fraser? The promo opportunities would have been amazing.'

Steph found herself thinking what a shame it was for Jack that he hadn't known of this earlier, but the marketing opportunities for promoting Glen Muir had been lost now. Given the circumstances, it couldn't be helped.

'Last-minute change of plans,' said Fraser.

Greg explained, 'Fraser asked me months ago but my schedule was packed. Then an engagement was cancelled so I got an early flight to Scotland instead. So, how about dinner?' he added swiftly. 'I was going to head south but I think I'll stay — if you'll consider being my tour guide to the Highlands?'

As smooth as the charm was, it held no underlying sweetness. Right now there was only one man who was the hero of the day for her — and he was a doctor, presumed missing in action on account of him hiding from fuss and adulation. In comparison Greg couldn't compete.

Steph smiled as she answered, 'For one, I'm not a local and for two, I've other arrangements, but thanks for the offer.'

Greg looked back at Steph in open incredulity. Clearly he wasn't used to being turned down, ever.

Without waiting for further chat, Steph turned away. 'I have to go and find Jack. If you see him, tell him to page me.'

And seconds later she had vanished, leaving Greg Fitzgerald staring after her, boggling at being sidelined.

⋆ ⋆ ⋆

Jack tapped Steph lightly on the shoulder. 'Come on, Events Woman Extraordinaire. You look exhausted — come with me, let me take you away from all this.'

Steph looked around her. People were chatting and laughing, some were picnicking around blankets and cool boxes, many indulging in the hog roast positioned nearby. There were children playing, balloons streaming vividly behind them, their face paint resplendent in the gathering dusk. The fair had been a resounding success, drawing a steady stream of visitors; Steph had never imagined the event would be quite so big.

Jack was still watching her with patience and an encouraging expression on his handsome features.

She shrugged her shoulders and

motioned to their surroundings. 'There's still clearing-up to do.' She pushed her hair away with the back of her arm. He snagged her fingers and pulled and she allowed him to lead her away.

'And that's what I pay the groundsmen for.' His smile could have tempted her to anything, even a double chocolate sundae during a bikini diet, he was that good.

They walked in the deepening twilight to the lochside. The air smelled of sweet greenery and fresh earth and the water looked like a magical fairytale backdrop.

'Is this a favourite spot for contemplation?' she inquired.

Jack bent for a pebble. 'I like to skim stones. I'm a dab hand at it, too. I reckon if it became an Olympic sport I'd be famous.'

Steph joined him on the shingle. Stuffing her hands in her cargo pants pockets, she tried not to look at him as much as she wanted to. 'You were amazing today.'

'So were you. However did we manage before you came?'

'You're forgetting you had Ally, queen of all she surveys and the woman who never admits defeat.'

'Except when baby decrees that mother needs rest.'

'There is that, true.'

'Of course, you do realise that when the baby comes, she and Fraser will be very occupied and I'll need a good second in command. Interested?'

'You're not serious?'

'Deadly. You're a natural, you're in need of work, I think we make a good team . . . do you need any more reasons?'

How about that I'm falling for you way too fast and way too deeply? Steph thought.

Jack walked over to her and took her hands from her pockets, entwining his fingers into hers. She saw the fullness of his lips, the jut of his masculine profile, those burly shoulders.

'A good team at work, a team with

potential,' he said softly.

'Potential for what? Rain clouds and disaster?' she retorted.

His eyes looked reproachful when he slotted his fingers between hers. 'You always disparage me, Steph. Actually I was thinking more along the lines of . . . love?'

Steph gasped. His directness shook her and almost made her topple. 'Are you serious?'

'Very serious. Life's been amazing since you got here. I don't want you to leave. I want to keep you here as long as I can.'

Steph blew out a sigh of shock; this was fast. 'Love isn't something that I readily add to my CV,' she mumbled. 'Once bitten, twice shy and all that . . .'

'Tell me about it.'

So she did. She started slowly at first — background, the years she'd spent with Charlie, how she'd been swept off her feet by the dashing London surgeon and he'd romanced her like no other man had. Then she gave brief clips about the dark part — his gambling, his drinking — the hidden side to a man she'd thought had been so erect, so principled.

His online debts had soon exceeded her yearly salary but still he wouldn't stop. He hadn't seen that he had a problem and yet his casino habit would have shocked a wealthy socialite and his yearning for a thrill and for money knew no bounds.

And it had slowly ground what little love she'd had left for him into the dust.

All the time he'd been lying, keeping it hidden lest his hallowed career should suffer from the tarnished reputation such a secret compulsion would bring. Steph had felt as if she was the only one that knew his secret; information she'd rather never have known.

Jack stared at her. 'I'm so sorry, Steph, I'd no idea.'

'And I prefer it that way. Especially the part where he died on a scooter in Greece after a huge row about money and debts, when I told him I intended to leave him.

'He yelled at me and went off in a rage and he never came back. In his view he didn't have a problem and he wasn't in the wrong. I keep the accident strictly under wraps — when people think your fiancé died in a bike crash they want to offer sympathy, but it's not sympathy for Charlie I want — it's explanations, such as why did he do it to me? Why wasn't I enough? Why was I just a foil for his self-interests?'

Jack pulled her close and his arms felt like a fortress that nothing could penetrate, so calming that she simply sighed and relished the comfort. 'You were a hero today,' she said.

He pushed her slightly away from him and sighed. Steph felt he was going to say something but was mulling it over. Not being held by him suddenly felt like a loss. She'd been savouring his arms around her, his strength and the warmth of his body.

His voice was low when he spoke.

'I'm no hero, Steph. Unfortunately that's where you're wrong . . . '

* * *

Jack took her with him to the long log on the water's edge.

The sound of the water lapping on the shingle and the occasional noises of night insects on nocturnal adventures were the backdrop to Jack's initial silence.

'There are things about me you should know,' he began softly. 'Because I sense there's mutual attraction and I want to be honest with you. I need you to be clear that I'm a guy who doesn't usually just jump headlong into a relationship and I have good reasons for that. But you're special and I want there to be something between us . . . I just have to tread with care . . . '

A swift flicker of alert sparked inside Steph's heart.

It had never occurred to her before this point, but Jack had told her he was single — yes, he'd told her that day when Hilary Benson had driven off in a rage. But now his words made her search her memory for clues, and for a moment she wondered if he was going to tell her he had a partner or ex in the picture.

'You're not with someone already?' she asked.

Jack looked puzzled. 'No, though I was engaged, and when it broke off I avoided dating like the plague . . . vowed I was off women forever. That's what happens when your heart feels as if it's been mugged.'

Inside Jack it was as if an old box with a rusty iron lock was opening — his own personal Pandora's box, and something he rarely broached with anyone. With Steph it was different; he wanted her to know. Yet it didn't lessen the pain of opening up old scars for discussion.

Jack played with her fingers, letting the tip of his own finger glide up and down each of hers in turn. He noticed her shiver — was that his touch or the light lochside breeze?

Indeed his head was whirling and his heart was beating fast from both the impact of the woman beside him and the implications of what he was about to reveal. If he was Steph and heard what had happened, would he bolt for the exit before anything even started?

Eventually he said, 'Paula dumped me a week before our wedding. She'd fallen in love with someone else, she said, and in the version I got at the time, she was filled with remorse for letting things go so far.'

'Had you both grown apart?'

'I suppose the signs were there. Perhaps I ignored them?'

'Sometimes it's hard to see . . . '

'We'd been arguing and not as close, but I presumed it was the pressure of wedding preparation. Suddenly the groom wasn't as important as the planning for the big day with the dress and all the arrangements. I figured it was just something couples go through when they're planning the biggest and most expensive day of their lives.

'Unfortunately I just didn't realise there was another man taking up her attentions, spending time with her in secret, quietly and stealthily making his move . . . '

'Drifting apart doesn't have to be over the stresses of a wedding. My own relationship drifted apart and I had no wedding to blame. It happens.'

Jack squeezed her hand, then with his other hand gently reached out to tuck her hair behind her ear.

'Paula sent me a letter with the old, 'It's not you, it's me,' line. But none of that was the real kick in the teeth, because the man she was leaving me for was Hamish, my own brother and best man, the man I'd've trusted with my life. He'd returned from Afghanistan a big soldier hero — one look and she'd known she'd chosen too soon and tied herself to the wrong brother.'

Jack had been left with two long letters of apology; one from Paula and one from Hamish.

'Who wants to read a lot of apologies that add up to nothing when the couple are prepared to run rough-shod over you anyway? They both left Glen Muir and went off to Australia — Sydney. Not that I've ever opened any letters from them — I see the frank and stamp and I bin them.'

Steph looked truly stunned by what he'd revealed. 'That must've been so hard for you to come to terms with.'

'I blocked it all out, I suppose.' He shrugged broad shoulders and shoved his dark emotions back in the box where he told himself they belonged. 'My father never knew Paula dumped me. I never told him. Hamish was his golden boy.'

Jack knew the real reasons that he'd hidden things. He'd been so drunk then he hadn't known up from down, taking solace, dulling the pain in a bottle and self-loathing. He still cursed himself for that crazy period of alcoholic haze — and he a doctor who prescribed lectures to others on addiction!

Jack looked deep into Steph's eyes. 'I drank to ease the mess my life was in. I even stole Dad's best antique malt — and I'm talking investment whisky, here, like setting a taper to hundred-pound notes. But the pain didn't taste any better on a malt that should've been in a museum.'

Steph laid her head gently on his shoulder. 'Didn't your dad help you through it?'

'Dad thinks Hamish is running a restaurant abroad. He had no idea they ran off to get away from me and to be together.'

'They weren't running from you, Jack; they ran from their own consciences,' Steph said staunchly. 'Sometimes the hardest thing is admitting you had no blame. It's easier to justify things with selfish reasons. Hamish and Paula deceived themselves.'

'At the time I handed in my notice at the practice and just lay in bed and hid away all day. So I'm no hero. I'm just a guy who reached rock bottom, then slowly picked himself up, took up the reins that Hamish left abandoned and realised the only person who could make it better was me.

'I turned my back on the bottle. I'm teetotal now, though I don't make a big deal of it; you probably haven't noticed the only drinks I have are soft ones.'

The strain on Jack's face was evident to Steph. She ached to just pull him close and kiss away his pain. The man deserved so much better. 'And your job — you got it back?'

'Luckily I have understanding partners. They gave me compassionate leave and let me return. I'll always be grateful.'

'I'm so sorry for what you've endured.'

'And I'm sorry about the motorbike incident you've been through . . . I didn't want to probe.'

Steph shrugged. 'He didn't jilt me. We were engaged but he kept putting off a wedding date — I know why now; he was slowly eating away at our nest egg. Charlie was ripping off me and his family to get the money to fuel his habit. It was an illness, I suppose,' she said wearily.

Jack laid his head back, as if he was tired and remembering exhausted him. Steph knew exactly how that felt. It hurt in every pore of your being, and with it came the blame and the doubt, making you wonder if you could ~~you~~ have seen it coming earlier.

'What kind of idiot lets down an amazing, beautiful woman like you and forsakes her for money?' He reached out his hand and touched her cheek.

She found herself cupping that hand to pull him closer. His touch caused every part of her to yearn for him. It would be so easy, too easy, to give in to the chemistry.

Jack leaned forward, his eyes sparkling. 'The thing is, you're different and, while it scares me, I can't ignore it. Can you handle interest from a guy who might get jealous or overprotective? I'm not jealous by nature, just wary from past experiences gone wrong.'

'Yes, Jack, I could handle it. Could you deal with a woman whose trust went up in smoke?'

He pulled her to him gently, his lips brushed hers and the promise of their kiss soothed her senses into bliss.

'Stephanie Baxter, you've no idea how much I want to try,' he murmured as he leaned towards her. He'd known it since they'd first met, known that this spark lurked, ready to burn bright — and what a spark!

Waves of pleasure surged through him as she kissed him back, revelling in the sensation, feeling his senses stir with quickening speed. She thrilled and tortured him simultaneously as his hands explored her curves.

A soft moan escaped her and he kissed her harder, slaking his need, then felt her pull slightly apart from him. He breathed deeply as he watched the confusion mixed with desire in the depths of her eyes.

'Steph, I've had to endure not daring to kiss you. I just couldn't any longer . . . '

She looked at him with longing and unvoiced questions. Then she bit her lip and moved slightly back.

'You feel the chemistry, too, don't you?' he implored.

'Enough for a block of science labs, I'd say!' She sighed.

That was another thing he loved about Stephanie Baxter. In the heat of anger, the depths of confusion or the midst of passion, she was able to laugh away any awkwardness and it endeared her to him in a way that went straight to his heart.

'We should take things slowly,' she said levelly. 'We both have past scars. As a doctor you know emotional wounds take the longest to heal.'

Jack looked at her. 'True. Not being a heart specialist and just a humble GP, what do you suggest we do about it?'

'A few dates, walks by the loch, dinner?' she suggested. 'Getting to know each other much better. Maybe lunch or a day out if we can fit it into our busy schedules?'

He smiled. 'I'm liking the sound of your prescribed advice.'

Steph jabbed him playfully in the ribs and again Jack found himself kissing her, this time dotting her temple with tiny butterfly touches.

'So I'm under doctor's orders to be steady and slow and give myself time?' His tone was husky with desire.

'That's about the size of it.'

'Then perhaps I'll have to be more creative with my pursuit.'

'Meaning?'

'Just wait and see . . . '

She pulled him back towards her by the front of his shirt. 'One more kiss, please. It's medicinal.'

He obliged without complaint, and it was several wonderful minutes before Steph was able to speak.

'Kissing you was about the only good

thing I did this evening,' she murmured. 'But I really have to say goodnight now, Jack.'

And she turned and left him standing there, watching her as she disappeared into the darkness.

12

It felt surreal, kissing Jack passionately and then disappearing off into the night alone. Steph had sighed wistfully after she'd walked back to the hotel, and had even watched through her window as he drove off.

And then reality dawned and she'd kicked herself — what was she thinking about? Would she even get another chance with a man like Jack? He was probably driving home mocking her ice-maiden aloofness and writing her off as too much like hard work.

Steph had little doubt that she'd wanted to kiss him with every fibre of her being, but sense had to take precedence. There were too many good relationships at stake here if she let them both charge in with their hormones blazing.

* * *

The next two days went by in a whirlwind of new arrivals at Abercarrick; a party of international golf enthusiasts from varied destinations had flown in, causing increased workloads.

Steph hadn't caught sight of Jack for those two days, even though she'd often cast hopeful glances, seeking his familiar tall presence on her tours of Glen Muir. Was he simply tied up with business, as she was, or was he trying to avoid her?

During a brief break on the third day, she put in her second call home to make sure her plans were in place.

'You've done it?' she asked in surprise. 'Mum you're an absolute star. So quickly — you don't hang around.'

Steph had only called her the day before to ask her to arrange for a friend to pack up some of her personal belongings and make enquiries at local letting agencies. Now her mother advised her that her friend had just lost a tenant and had a room going spare in her own house. It was just a few streets away from Steph's current flat.

'That's fantastic.'

'Anyway, I've sent a holding deposit to her for you. You're sure you won't reconsider our offer, love? We'd happily give you a deposit to buy your own place. It might be small, given London prices, but it would be yours.'

'No, Mum — I need that money you withdrew for me. The savings plus my redundancy will make a big difference. Ally and Fraser need help, right now, and I intend to offer it. If Jenny needs a flatshare it feels like kismet,' Steph declared.

At last some things were starting to go right again.

Her friends' business was in jeopardy and Steph felt she could help. At times like this it was good that her parents trusted her judgement. Certainly she'd known Ally and Fraser for years but investing thousands of pounds in a business, however close the ties were, wasn't something she'd normally condone.

'Your father says you're doing the right thing,' her mother said. 'He says there's a cheque in the post to you, too. He wants to give you something to add to the coffers. Says he knows what it was like when he was young and starting out on his own; small businessmen need to stick together. We trust your judgement, love, and we want to help.'

Steph was taken aback. 'No, don't go sending money. I'm not looking for you to pitch in,' she protested.

'You'll do what's necessary to pull things together with it.' Glenda Baxter could be incredibly stubborn when she felt like it and Steph knew when to give in.

'Thank you,' she said humbly. 'You're amazing, you know that?' Her heart swelled with pride.

'Steph,' Glenda said, trying to mask the emotion in her voice and failing miserably. 'We're so pleased you're getting on with things, love — putting the past behind you . . . ' There was a long pause as her mother pulled herself together. Steph could hear her blowing her nose at the other end of the line and knew she would be dabbing at her eyes.

'Don't get upset, Mum, please.'

'Hear me out. Deep down you know Charlie would've said what I'm going to say to you now . . . ' Steph waited, her heart drumming in her chest, holding her breath.

'You have to push yourself and take risks, Stephie. There's more to life than memories, much more.'

But Steph knew Charlie's dark side, too, and in spite of the fact that she'd loved him once, he'd been capable of hurting her deeply. This was the side of Charlie that Glenda and Steph's father, Alec, never saw. It was the side Steph had never confided to them. She and Jack weren't so very different at heart; they'd both kept dirty secrets to protect the ones they loved the most.

She didn't want to think about the past or Charlie — about the way he'd used her, the way he'd lied, the years he'd covered up and mistreated her.

Steph's own eyes were swimming with tears now and they ran freely down her face. 'I know. It's time to move on, Mum. And that's what I'm doing now.'

* * *

Jack had worn his father's sedate grey and white silk tie for luck but it wasn't proving so lucky; he just felt suffocated by the stiff shirt collar. He always felt at his most uncomfortable in business suits and would much rather be in full Highland rig-out than in pinstripes.

'Your business plan shows clever thinking, Jack. I appreciate the marketing plan isn't ready yet, but a word of warning on that; don't be too ambitious in your plans,' his bank manager told him. Jack and Terry Dunbar had known each other for years; their relationship was built on long-earned trust. 'The security issue won't work as things stand.'

Terry sighed; it was difficult to have to come down hard on Jack's hopes. 'The revenue projections you've put forward are ambitious. You must know this yourself.'

Jack looked at the report in front of him and nodded, knowing 'ambitious' was an understatement, but he had to try.

'I've researched the figures,' he pointed out. 'You know how committed we are to doing all we can to drive the business forward. But I do understand your concerns.'

'You have secured loans already.' Terry got up and paced the floor. 'If we base more funding on a too-ambitious business plan that doesn't materialise, it will spell disaster.'

Jack could plainly see it troubled Terry to have to say it.

Terry offered Jack another coffee and poured himself one.

'The bank's official position is that security alone is not enough to ensure backing. This plan needs to be water-tight. I'm prepared to give you half, but that's my very best offer. Times are tight, Jack — I'm really sorry.'

Jack's jaw was firm. He pushed the cup and saucer away and reined in his impatience, but if he were honest, it was as much as he could have expected.

'I'd suggest you get private backing somehow. Limit your expansion plans to what will have the best return.' Terry shuffled with the papers awkwardly and added, 'We've discussed this issue before, Jack but have you considered selling land to private developers?'

Jack's briskly determined head-shake announced that it wasn't even worth voicing a reply.

'Can you find the extra money?' Terry asked. 'Perhaps finding another partner would the best way forward.'

Jack stood up and looked out of the window into the busy London city street below.

'I'll find the money. I appreciate this offer and intend to take it, so I'll come back when I've secured the rest — I just have more work to do first.'

Terry reached into his desk drawer and took out a card. 'We're friends, Jack. Try these people — my contact is a venture capitalist. He may just be looking for something to add to his portfolio. No promises, but worth a try while you're in London.'

'I'll do that.' Jack pocketed the card.

They shook hands, exchanging looks that said they understood the pressures on each of them, then Jack turned and left the office.

★ ★ ★

According to anyone Steph asked about Jack, he was away on business and had had to go urgently. Fortunately she was too busily occupied by work to mope.

The lunchtime trade in the Glen Muir Highlander Bar made it the busiest shift of the day but Steph barely noticed. She'd been moved to bar waitressing duty since she'd offered to muck in wherever there was a vacant slot that needed filling. She was widening her hotel horizons in lots of ways.

The hotel attracted regular lunchtime visitors. The fact that it also had fantastic views meant that it was a natural stopping-off point for tourers. In the high tourist season this lunch-time trade necessitated expansion of the dining room into the adjoining parlour bar. Visitors could sit and marvel at the stunning view of the loch and hills beyond, in a bona fide picture postcard view.

Steph enjoyed being busy, and running around doing an assortment of varied tasks kept her fully occupied; afterwards she felt as if she'd done a workout.

'This place keeps you fit, huh?' said Kylie, passing by as she showed a couple of guests to the restaurant.

Jess, Steph and Kylie had already

shared girly nights over a bottle of Merlot or an old black and white movie, and Steph looked forward to her regular visits. Her London life suddenly seemed distant — and yet she'd been in Abercarrick for hardly any time at all.

Clearing a table at super-speed and with plates stacked up her arm, she became aware of suspicious giggling from one of the bar's nooks and went to investigate.

In the dark corner a couple were talking conspiratorially and the woman of the pair kept stifling laughter. Steph immediately recognised Jack's long athletic legs stretched out. Her heart bottomed out, her pulse soared. He was back — and not only has he not even bothered to come and find her, but now he was with another woman having a nice, cosy time together!

Realising she couldn't back off now, Steph rounded the partition and found Jack sitting cosily on a snug bench with a stunning blonde. She was the most wonderful-looking woman Steph had ever seen, with long, straight blonde tresses, glittering baby-blue eyes and a smile that could stop motorway traffic. Just your regular modern-day Helen of Troy — and she had her hand on Jack's arm.

Steph's peace of mind evaporated. For days he'd been missing, and now he was suddenly dating a supermodel!

Steph knew that the smile had faltered on her lips but she pushed ahead and introduced herself. 'Hello. Can I get you good people anything?' She thrust out two menus, almost wishing she could hit them both in the faces with them.

'Steph.' Jack sat up straight in his seat and the laughter left his eyes. 'Great to see you.'

'Have you ordered or can I tell you about our specials?' Steph took solace in just doing the job. It was easier than explanations, easier than running — and much, much preferable to ranting and raving and demanding why he'd kissed her and where he'd been. But she just couldn't help herself and glared at him as she spoke.

'We have Two Timer Toasties, Gone Without Explanation Paninis, New Totty On The Scene Salads and Never Dare To Kiss Me Again Jacket Potatoes.' Her eyes flashed defiance.

Jack had both shock and laughter in his eyes when he finally parried back with, 'Have you met my little sister?'

Steph's jaw dropped and she just stared at him, trying not to drop her order pad.

'Marnie's just arrived from the Caribbean. I went to London to pick her up. I had a medical conference to attend so we combined the two.'

'My brother's been telling me all about you,' said Marnie, offering Steph a manicured and bejewelled hand to shake.

Steph found herself fighting to control the blush that had taken over her entire body. She had been looking hopefully at the double doors every time someone walked in, hoping hard for Jack, and now she'd gone and turned their reunion into a complete embarrassment.

Steph took her hand. 'Oh, hi. I know I look a little old for work experience but that's basically what I'm doing here. Jack's teaching me the hotel trade from the bottom up, and I'm toiling my way around all the departments.'

Marnie played with the dazzling silver necklace at her tanned collarbone. 'I'm back because of you, actually, Steph. Jack says there's an opportunity in the spa and as I'm a beautician we're back in business as a team again! You and I must meet later on and get to know each other properly. Come over to Jack's place later — I'll protect you from him,' Marnie said, rising from her table. 'He's a pussycat really. You just have to get to know how to work him right.'

'Great . . . em . . . see you later, then.' Steph considered that perhaps she didn't want protecting from Marnie's brother at all, and she was also secretly pleased to get a chance to visit Jack's home territory.

'Oh — Steph?' Marnie looked back over her shoulder with a wry grin. 'I really like the sound of those Don't Dare To Kiss Me Again Jacket Potatoes. They sound hot — especially as I suspect Jack's been sampling your menu already.'

Steph scurried away, wishing she could undo the damage her mouth had done — but with a glimmer of fresh excitement at the evening ahead.

As she rushed off, head down, knowing she was still blushing crimson from her faux pas with Jack's sister, she heard someone call her name.

'Steph, wait up. It's me, Jack.'

She pulled the scraps of her pride together and turned to face him. 'I'd been wondering where you were — ever the man of mystery, aren't you?'

'Miss me any?' he asked, his expression tugging at her heart and her impulses.

Only like a missing limb, she

thought. She'd had to stop herself thinking about him every moment of every day. Who wouldn't have their head turned by a guy who'd kissed her so ably then disappeared without a word of explanation?

'A little,' Steph lied with a noncommittal shrug. 'Anyway, I've wanted to speak to you for ages about the hotel marketing issues — I've had lots of thoughts and ideas and we still haven't discussed things fully.'

'I had to go to London, Steph. I had business to attend to. Unfortunately it's not as good news as I'd hoped and they can't give me the money I'd asked for — or at least, not enough. So marketing might have to go on hold.'

'But surely it's the lifeline that can save the hotel?'

Jack shook his head. 'True, if cash reserves were no object, but they are and I've been warned to be sensible.'

'As it happens I've been doing some thinking on that. Can we discuss it soon? I've written you a document you can use and I've costed out lots of ideas.'

'Sure, though I'm not sure I'll be able to afford much. We'll talk soon. Personally I'm more interested in those previous discussions we had about 'slow dating'. How about we concentrate on that?'

He walked toward her and pulled her to him; his grasp was warm, his body ensnaring and hard to resist.

But Steph felt blind-sided by his jump in topic, just as she had been when she'd found him in the bar's cosiest nook with a woman. This guy was still capable of surprising her, catching her off-balance, and that whittled away at her trust.

It felt as if he was sidelining the hotel — his dreams, his business — and focusing only on their fledgling interest in each other. Was that all he cared about, or was he hiding his business head in the sand?

'I'll think about it,' Steph rebuffed him swiftly. 'And once you set up a date for a business meeting I'll take you seriously in return. I've done a lot of work for you with no expectation but I'm saddened to think you dismiss it so readily.' She pulled away sharply. 'I've got to go. I'm working — or hadn't you noticed?'

She turned and disappeared into the kitchen, suddenly wishing she hadn't been so snippy with Jack, but feeling that somehow, somewhere along the line, they'd crossed wires — and he wasn't taking her involvement in Glen Muir as seriously as she'd believed he would.

Steph was suddenly filled with even more conviction — she'd impress Jack McGregor and Fraser and Ally and make them see she was right, and that she was of some value to them and to the business.

When she got the chance, Jack would realise just how much she cared about Glen Muir — and how her involvement was vital if their fortunes were to be saved.

13

Jack turned to see Steph's car appearing in his driveway. She emerged looking bright and vivacious as only she could. Her hair shone like a halo and her smile touched his heart. She turned to survey the place and closed the car door behind her.

She'd left him earlier with a flea in his ear, and he jumped over the picket fence to get to her first in case she stalked off.

'Hi.' He walked across the driveway, smiling. 'This is what I call a pleasant surprise. What are you doing in my backyard?' Jack gave her a brief hug of welcome that told her he meant it.

She was dressed down but in flirty style with a black off-the-shoulder top and snug jeans. He had to hold himself back from kissing the shoulder on display.

'I'm here to see Marnie. She invited me over, remember — is that okay?' Steph looked around her, taking in Jack's home, a small worker's cottage on the very edge of the estate; tranquil, practical, low-key and very homely.

Jack had secretly been hoping to organise a secluded dinner for two as soon as business affairs let him — but now Marnie had beaten him to it. He really wanted to steer Steph away for a stroll in the opposite direction but with a resigned shrug, he knew he'd have to do the decent thing.

'I'd better take you to find little sis then,' he said, 'but before we do, we've unfinished business.' He gently reminded her of exactly where they'd left off by the loch. It was a repeat performance he'd been very much saving himself for. Somehow he'd managed to forget, during his years of restrained celibacy, that kissing could be very good indeed — and fortunately her response indicated she seemed to feel the same way too.

* * *

Bright stars blazed in Steph's mind and comets could have been colliding above them and she wouldn't have even noticed. She was on a distant planet somewhere north of Venus after having been kissed by Jack. Her feet barely touched terra firma and suddenly all her earlier gripes were forgotten.

'You okay?' he gave her a sidelong glance as he led her to the renovated cottage he called home.

Steph felt a frisson of excitement as she walked beside him, enjoying his tall frame shadowing hers.

Jack caught her hand on the doorstep. 'I'm sorry I've been so wrapped up in work. I wanted to drop by and see you before I left, but there wasn't time. I had to sort out hotel finances. I tried calling, but you were always busy.'

Steph suddenly noted the tired lines that proved he'd been burning the candle at both ends. 'You look like you've had too much on your plate for sanity's sake.'

'Business has been pressing, to say the least,' he replied.

'I must confess I did think you'd seen the light and gone off me, but it's okay. I've been busy being your employee of the week. Apparently I'm an exceptional receptionist, and an even better waitress. Jess told me, twelve out of ten — impressed?'

Jack's smile was melt-worthy as he bent to kiss her again to confirm his approval. She'd been dying to see him again and couldn't wait to start putting their earlier doubts behind them. In spite of it, though, she still had enough feminine wiles at her disposal to prevent her diving at him like a love-lorn desperado.

'So when can I see you again?' he asked eagerly.

'Sorry,' she said with a smile. 'I have an awful boss — you probably know him ... great big scary chap, goes by the name McGregor The Terrible

. . . work always takes precedence.'

Jack groaned and she felt him regard her casual attire intently. The desire-filled look in his eyes told her the next kiss was going to slay her attempts to play it flirty and cool.

But they were rudely interrupted.

'Hi, Steph, great to see you!' Marnie enthused, stopping Jack in his tracks. She'd emerged clad in the tightest of tight shorts and bikini top, an ensemble that made her look as if she'd jumped fresh from a magazine cover. 'Jack, the ice-machine's broken. Can you fix it for me?'

They walked together into a large airy kitchen devised via a large glass extension to the rear of the cottage.

Jack cast a look that told of frustration and waning tolerance and Steph handed over a bag of gourmet goodies.

'I brought food,' she told Marnie. 'I raided Fraser's larder.'

What Abercarrick may lack in nearby off-licences and supermarkets it made up for with Fraser's pantry; marinated chicken, dressed olives, stuffed quail's eggs and more gastro nibbles than a girl could possibly want.

Jack cast a pleading look at Steph while his sister was occupied with the treats.

'The ice machine, Jack,' Marnie urged. 'Did you hear me?'

Marnie summoned Steph to follow her out onto the deck beyond the French windows as Jack sloped off to do Marnie's bidding, grumbling as he went.

The views from the deck were fantastic, but it seemed Marnie's mood didn't match.

'I'm so fed up,' Marnie said, rummaging for a tissue.

'Don't get upset,' Steph urged. 'What's so bad?'

'I fell out with my boyfriend and stormed off the cruise ship I was working on — and now I'm having second thoughts.'

'I thought you were keen to start

work at Glen Muir again?' Steph probed as she took an olive. Agony aunt was not exactly her chosen vocation and she felt a little awkward.

Marnie shook her head. 'I know, but I love Marios. Maybe I simply misjudged him? I thought he was having a fling but he assured me it was all just a misunderstanding.'

'Come on,' Steph said, putting her hand on Marnie's. 'Why don't you call him and explain? But you also need to talk to your brother about your commitment to Glen Muir.'

'Jack won't listen. He won't let me go back to Marios.'

'I think your brother is wary because he cares for you. Maybe he'd change his mind if Marios could come here and prove the strength of his affections? Big brothers are supposed to look out for their little sisters, you know — I have one myself.'

Steph smiled. 'Plus there's another thing — don't you realise that your brother might appreciate your help with the hotel right now? As much as your heart is pulling you away, Jack could really use another pair of hands right now,' Steph said, practically-minded as ever.

Marnie twisted the crumpled tissue in her lap. 'I didn't realise Jack needed me. I suppose if Marios came here then at least he'd be away from that floozie dancer on the ship, but then, maybe you're right and I need time to think and cool off.'

Steph sighed and slumped back in her seat just as Jack reappeared bearing a bucket of ice, noticed his sister's tear-heavy eyes and left the room again, giving Steph a puzzled look but saying nothing.

Marnie lowered her voice conspiratorially. 'So, how come my brother lights up like a Christmas tree when you're in the room?'

Steph avoided her gaze. 'He took me to see Ally in hospital and we've become friends, but right now that's not important. I need your help before you go off romancing your cruise liner beau again, Marnie. I'm designing ads for the hotel and you used to be a model — I can't offer you a single penny for doing it, but would you pose for photographs?'

Marnie looked genuinely dumb-struck; Steph herself knew it was a shot in the dark. 'Of course I will,' Marnie replied. 'Especially if it'll help my brother's business; he's been pacing the floor all night about it lately.'

Marnie grinned as she continued, 'In fact, I can go even better . . . let me pull some strings and do you a proper professional job.' she added, 'I know a photographer who might help us out.' Marnie McGregor did nothing by halves.

'But I need this all quickly and I've no budget,' Steph replied anxiously. 'I mean it, Marnie — this is an SOS project — and you can't tell Jack about it yet.'

Marnie took her Blackberry from the table and dialled. 'I can fix it. The world runs on favours. But there is one condition,' she said with a finger resting on rosy lips. 'You tell me what's going on between you and Jack first, and then I'll say yes.'

Steph took a deep breath. These McGregors drove hard bargains indeed.

* * *

It was growing dusky when Steph told Marnie she'd have to get back to the hotel. She made her way over the gravel searching for the keys that she knew were in her bag, but wouldn't surface.

She reached the car and the hairs on the back of her neck prickled with the kind of unease that earned strangled violin sound effects in films. The unmistakable crack of branches underfoot sounded behind her and sent her pulse racing. There was definitely someone there.

A warm hand slid around her waist, and she would have screamed were it not for Jack's whisper beside her ear.

'It's okay. It's only me.'

'I should knee you somewhere painful for this. You nearly gave me a coronary.'

'Then you're in safe hands.' Jack slid her around to face him. 'Because I'm the local doctor.'

The familiar citrus smell and touch of his hands were delicious. She'd missed him so much. That deep awareness gushed inside her and she knew in her heart that she really wanted time with him, to let the new feelings she had flourish.

But she pushed the thoughts down, knowing there were more important things that had to be dealt with first. 'I need to talk to you, Jack. I've been having lots of thoughts and working on my own proposals for the hotel. Can we meet to talk about them?'

'Absolutely. Dinner tomorrow.'

'No.' Steph shook her head, firm in her own conviction. It was one thing that she badly wanted to date Jack, but quite another when it came to her professional approach to work. She wanted a proper business meeting and wouldn't settle for less. 'A business lunch,' she suggested. 'Or even better, why don't I book us a conference room for the end of the week?'

'Sure, if that's what you want,' he murmured. 'Can I take you home now?' He looked dark and handsome; utterly appealing in black designer jeans and grey T-shirt.

'I need to see you, it's been too long,' he murmured, bending to kiss her exposed shoulder. 'You're stretching my patient nature to the limits.'

'It was you who went off to London.'

'No choice, sweetie. Work, work, work.'

Her heart was drumming frenzied pulsating beats in her chest. 'Is it wise, us sneaking about in the hotel?' she asked.

Jack kicked the gravel. 'Now Marnie's here I'm like a prisoner in my own home. I'd like some time with you solo.'

'I don't want us starting rumours at

Glen Muir, Jack.'

Jack gently held her face in his hands. 'Then next weekend we're going to escape Glen Muir. Leave it to me and I'll arrange it. I need to spend proper time with you, if you'll let me? Just the two of us, you and me. What do you say?'

He nuzzled her hair gently, moving the tendrils and kissing her forehead softly, his breath warm on her skin.

'I say yes, Jack . . . '

14

Steph felt incredibly nervous. Her mouth was dry and her palms itched. Her heart was doing a strange pitter-patter in her chest, and her stomach — well, she didn't even want to think about the limbo dance going on in there. She couldn't remember feeling this nervous for years.

Fraser arrived in the meeting room first. Her proposals — some displayed on mounted board — were placed around the vast polished table for inspection. Fraser went towards them and she held up a warning finger for him to wait. 'Not yet,' she said. She bade him take a seat, then rose to pour them coffee.

She'd arranged it all like a proper business proposals pitch with a Power-Point computer presentation, display boards, shortbread, Java coffee — the works.

Steph smoothed down her favourite dress — sent via post by her mother because it was her lucky frock — and hoped hard that it would help her.

She looked up just as Jack arrived, breezing in with a wide smile and looking gorgeous. She realised she badly wanted a hug to ease the nerves — but not in front of Fraser.

She carefully put a coffee in front of him with shaky hands, then took a long, deep breath. This was it — she had to be pitch perfect. Taking another calming breath, she turned to face them and began her presentation.

'Thanks for coming,' Steph said brightly. She summarised her findings; that there were two elements to her proposed marketing strategy for Glen Muir — namely weddings and women's pampering opportunities, and a second strand involving expansion of community partnerships.

She showed them the professional photographs of Jess and emphasised her views that Glen Muir was a fabulous, but currently under-utilised, venue for weddings. The disused chapel on the estate could be a real feather in their cap if they had the vision to restore it to use. Lavish Scottish-themed weddings would boom if they could market it properly.

In terms of opportunities for the spa, Steph summarised that while they had an extensive database of past customers, they should be mailing them discounts and offers on a regular basis.

'You should be proactive in keeping golfers and business guests as loyal customers, many of whom could bring partners to the spa if you offer them discounts and maximise packages to tempt them. Most business comes from existing customers and you need to start using your contact information as a marketing tool.'

Finally Steph revealed her most progressive idea — the disused stables block that had untapped potential.

The Highland fair had revealed just what Glen Muir could do with local involvement, and she suggested letting space out to the Simply Scottish Soap Store or even the local wedding photographer, who had told her he was currently struggling to find just the right new office space.

In addition, they should be considering gallery and coffee shop space as an add-on to a newly transformed stable annexe; a visitor centre that would bring more interest onto the estate.

'And what about the cookery demos you held at the fair?' she challenged Fraser. 'They attracted the biggest crowds and there's huge potential for that — how about culinary weekends for gastro foodies? This hotel has so many exciting opportunities it's staggering. It just needs a little work to make it flourish.'

Jack and Fraser stared at her hard enough for her to almost believe she'd sprouted a moustache. Suddenly she wondered if she was bombing with this. Had she pitched it wrong?

'I've been working on some initial

advertising proposals with the key objective being to increase Glen Muir's presence in relevant national press and to initiate some meaningful relationships with local companies that will enhance our profile and feed into a successful marketing push.'

She knew she sounded like a marketing wizard, even if she didn't quite feel like it. All those years at the helm of her old company had certainly stood her in good stead.

'This report,' she nodded to the papers laid out on the table before them, 'details target media for a concentrated four-month campaign. Not long, I know, but it should get us maximum exposure on minimum spend. Costings, deadlines and provisionally negotiated deals are detailed in the appendix but I think you'll agree the deals I've already struck can't be bettered.

'I've space on hold and have a budget to run with these immediately. I also have a promotional brochure for the spa at final proof stage, ready for database-wide mailing. I can go live with new web pages for the spa and weddings at Glen Muir immediately — once given the green light, that is.'

Jack looked as if he needed to pick his jaw up off the floor and she started to wonder if she'd flopped dismally. Fraser flicked through the pages and gave a concerned headshake.

'Steph,' he said with a grave voice, 'I don't mean to quash you but I did mention before . . . ' he scanned through the chart of costs, 'This is advertising money we just don't have.' He looked at Jack for agreement and moved awkwardly in his seat. 'I wish I'd stopped you sooner.'

Jack scanned the report with a face that gave nothing away then his dark eyes regarded Fraser with a hard glare.

Steph took a deep breath, cleared her throat and said quickly, 'I appreciate that, which is why I'd like to put forward the money myself. I have redundancy money and savings and I'd like to invest it in Glen Muir.'

It was disconcerting having Jack McGregor watching her every move so intently. She tried to still her racing heartbeat in order to proceed, giving him an almost reproachful look.

'The money has cleared and is sitting in my bank account. Say yes, and we can get moving immediately on this. I think it's a sound investment — I always say you should back a good cause when you believe strongly in it. I've discussed this with Ally and she's in agreement.'

Fraser and Jack simply looked at her, stunned. It seemed that Steph had succeeding in silencing them both simultaneously.

'This is staggering!' Jack said, regarding her with a look little short of wonder. 'But, Steph, we can't take your money.'

Jack moved to his feet in order to pick up her draft adverts, read their copy and peruse her work. He nodded his head on seeing the graphics she'd prepared for her suggested partnership with the local soap shop owner.

'She needs extra premises,' Steph pointed out. 'We've had no firm discussions yet, but I know she'd be interested in the spare accommodation here.' Steph lowered her voice and said softly, 'And the money is yours, Jack.'

'No — it's my problem,' Jack declared emphatically. 'But nevertheless, this really is great work.'

Steph stared long, hard and meaningfully at Jack.

'You're an amazing woman,' Jack said and throwing caution aside pulled her to him and kissed her warmly in front of Fraser.

Just then Jack's mobile trilled into action. 'Hold on a minute.' He scanned the text on his mobile with a look of utter shock. 'We'll talk again tonight. I have to go. I'll see you later.'

And he was off without explanation, like a sprint runner.

After the highs of the morning, Steph felt deflated.

'Well, that went down like a lead-filled

balloon,' she said, shaking her head. She slowly began to take down her carefully prepared presentation. So much for her hard work.

★ ★ ★

Jack burst into reception a short while later, clutching a bunch of flowers. Steph thought he might be getting carried away too soon. It wasn't exactly a celebration moment yet. The ads weren't a fail-safe answer to the hotel's problems; they were merely a means to try to steer them into calmer waters.

'I have backing — I just got word!' he said. 'Time to celebrate. And I didn't get time to thank you for all that amazing promotional work you've done. You are a genius. I love your ideas and I want to run with them all. So does Fraser!'

He twirled her round in a pirouette. She could feel the soft fabric of her dress revealing far too much thigh for her dignity.

'One of the things I had to do in London was to seek venture capital backing — and we've got it! — from a sleeping partner who owns an internet travel company. He has faith in us and wants to help us achieve our dreams with Glen Muir,' Jack said animatedly. 'I couldn't possibly take your money, and now I don't have to.'

'Why not? Surely it just means there's more in the pot now, to ensure that our plans come to fruition?'

'Because it's my problem and you need your money yourself. It's not up for discussion.'

'I knew it!' Steph pushed the flowers away in disgust. 'Jack the big brave hero can't take charity.'

'No, I'm looking after your interests,' he said, loosening the silk tie at his neck and removing his suit jacket. 'Maybe now the dust is settling I can sleep again. Unless of course you'd like to stay up tonight together?' His tone suggested that his mind was on things very far removed from business.

Steph had never seen Jack as animated. It was clear how much this meant to him.

'Well, I'm glad I could help, and once you get things going you'll have to keep in touch and let me know how it all panned out,' she said, trying to hide the hurt she was now feeling. He'd declined her money, found an alternative and now it felt as if she was no longer needed — other than as someone to flirt with.

'Oh, no you don't. That's my other big news — I want to contract you to undertake all your plans. There's no one better than the woman who came up with all the ideas to actually implement them. Name your salary and I'll fix up in a contract that meets your plans.'

Steph stared at him, shocked. 'You want me to work here?'

'Permanently, if you'd do it. Though I suppose it's not fair to ask you to make that kind of commitment. I'll fit in with whatever you can offer us.'

Steph could feel his warm hands through the thin fabric of her dress as he pulled her towards him and kissed her briefly, making her senses swim, her pulse accelerate and her insides do gymnastic flips.

'Life doesn't get better than this,' he whispered huskily into her ear. 'So you'd better start packing.'

'Pack for what?' she asked, almost stunned speechless at the suddenness of it all and struggling to keep up with the twists and turns of this conversation.

'Our escape, remember? And now it's a celebration combined. You'll need an overnight bag for the weekend,' Jack said, stroking the hair at the nape of her neck.

'I can't go.'

Of course she *wanted* to go; wild horses couldn't stop her wanting to, but there was more going on here than simply what she wanted.

'Why not?' Jack said, frustration marring his fine features.

It truly galled her that he wasn't even prepared to let her help with the money for advertising and just dismissed the suggestion so easily. How could he just dismiss her efforts? Didn't he see her proposition made perfect sense? She wasn't about to budge an inch.

'Because,' said Steph stiffly, 'until you agree to take my money for marketing, it's non-negotiable.' And with that she stormed off leaving Jack and her bouquet behind her.

★ ★ ★

As he turned to leave reception Jack saw that the door to the staffroom was open a tiny crack and one eye was beadily watching him. The door shut when he approached but he shoved a hand out and forced it open, revealing the eavesdropper.

'Enjoy the floor show, Jess?'

Jess stood looking meek and apologetic but there was something about her expression that told Jack she was more than a touch delighted.

'Sorry boss. Wrong place, wrong time.'

'Well, keep this business to yourself, will you?'

'Sure thing,' she answered, but she let out a low and meaningful whistle and tutted slowly to his retreating back.

Jack turned around and pointed an accusing finger. 'Jess, are you doing security shifts as well these days?'

'Dr McGregor,' she replied in clipped tones, 'you may be part owner here but I happen to be glad you've at last opened your eyes wide and found a love life. You may be my boss and my doctor, but your well-being is important to me, you know.'

Jess flounced off wearing a secret smile of such glee that for once Jack McGregor was without words.

But he also had to go and make the woman who'd impressed him most say yes to his proposal. As he rushed off to follow Steph, he took out his mobile phone and sent her a text.

Okay. I'm sorry and you win. I'm utterly at your mercy. Please just say yes.

15

Steph zipped up her tote bag with a bit of coercion; she'd stuffed a lot in there for her trip with Jack . . . well, a girl liked to be prepared. Jess had lent her some clothes as well as the tote bag to take them in, since all she'd brought was her large case and clothes that could only be described as comfy and casual at best.

Jess looked at her doubtfully. 'So, you're all prepared. You're definitely going to go now?'

'I am. It feels crazy and impulsive, but do I want to go! Jack and I never seem to get any time together, so this is a chance to see whether we gel.'

Steph sat down on Jess's comfy sofa beside her. The kids were in bed and Gordon was out at a darts competition.

'Can you do me a favour? Tell me more about Paula and Hamish?' Steph asked.

'Paula and Hamish? Now there's a tale,' Jess said, preparing for a long oratory. 'She broke Jack's heart; left him high and dry a week before the wedding. Apparently rumour has it she tried to get her bridesmaid to go and do the deed to avoid sullying her own fair hands.'

'He really loved her, did he? You told me before you could see through her?'

Jess expanded. 'She was classy, rich, American. She moved back here with Jack and was clearly unimpressed by Glen Muir life. Her trips to the States became more and more regular as time went on. I knew they were arguing and that Paula was keen for Jack to move to California and take up practice there. But Jack has strong bonds to hearth and home and he wasn't budging. It was like, the more he refused the more she got mad. Back home she was Daddy's little girl who got whatever she wanted, so this was something new to her.'

'And how did Hamish come into the picture?'

'He was the returning hero, just retired from the army. As soon as they were on the scene together they began flirting behind Jack's back, acting like something from a rom-com movie montage. Suddenly Paula's mind wasn't on wedding plans any more, but on the new talent in town.' Jess's features took on a hard and thoughtful expression. 'Or of course, maybe it was also the fact that Hamish is rightful heir of Glen Muir, not Jack?'

'You think she was mercenary?'

'Nothing would surprise me about her. But Hamish knew this estate just eats money, which is why he was keen to get away. I think she realised that if Jack refused to budge she'd be stuck here without as fine a bank balance as she craved.'

'Hamish is rich, then?'

'What isn't Hamish McGregor? He's confident, full of his own importance; he always seems to land on his feet and ends up smelling of roses no matter what, so I'm sure he's found a profitable niche in Australia somehow. I heard that he made a lot of money in property investment while he was in the army. He was always one to have several strings to his bow, and Paula wouldn't still be with him if he hadn't.'

'Jack told me he tried to keep Hamish's wrongdoings secret from his father . . . '

Jess looked at her with empathy for Jack's plight. 'Hamish was his father's favourite — the golden boy of Glen Muir — everyone knew that. Jack preferred to step away and ignore it, so it's no surprise he never told his father. Jack's loyal and decent in all the ways his brother is not; he shouldered the cancelled wedding on his own and kept it to himself.

'To this day the old Major probably thinks that Hamish is fault free. Little does he know that he's with Paula and they both walked all over Jack.'

Steph had her fingers pressed to her lips. Poor Jack!

'So he deserves to have a great

weekend with you, don't you think?' Jess probed plainly. 'The man's paid his dues.'

'Jess, it's early days, we barely know each other . . . '

'There's a spark as big as a Fourth of July parade between you two, and time's not a factor; I knew Gordon was the one within a week of us first meeting.'

'Which is why you'll always be a true romantic, Jess Cameron, and why I never will,' Steph replied dryly.

'By the way,' Jess added lifting her glass, 'you're staying here tonight. We've polished off a bottle and a half of wine already. I promised the boss I'd look after you.'

Lately Steph had felt a glow, and it had occurred at the hands of a handsome doctor not a million miles away. One who was taking her away tomorrow.

★   ★   ★

'Steph, wake up, you're dreaming,' Jess said urgently, shaking Steph awake. She was still on Jess's sofa and her chest was tight. As she fought for breath, she looked up to see Jess's worried face close to her own.

It was pitch dark and Jess's hair was tousled from sleep. 'You frightened me; it sounded like someone was hurting you.'

'I'm sorry . . . ' Steph felt the clammy heat of perspiration on her skin and her face hot.

Jess sat on the edge of the bed, 'I'm going to make us both some cocoa. Stay there.'

Steph tried to remember her dream but she already knew this was often futile. She knew from the exhaustion she felt that it had been another nightmare — and it must have been a particularly bad one to have woken her host.

Jess soon returned with a tray bearing steaming mugs.

'You were screaming, Steph, and it was horrific — are these the dreams you talked about, the ones about the accident?'

Steph explained in more detail about her flashbacks to the scooter accident.

'And I hate to ask it but . . . did this guy Charlie ever hit you?' Jess chewed her lip anxiously.

Steph shook her head. 'No. I was scared of him and sometimes his rages drove me to run away, but Charlie never hit me. Although he did spend all our money, and sold our furniture and my car. He took every ounce of patience and self-respect I had. He was cruel, and a gambler — but he wasn't violent.'

Jess let out a long low breath of relief.

'He killed himself, I know he did. There was no suicide note but — he killed himself because of what I said to him, Jess. I told him to go and never come back.'

The tears were streaming down her face now and Steph accepted Jess's offer of a warm embrace.

'You poor thing,' Jess said, hugging her and soothing her with a hand on her hair. 'It's hardly surprising you replay such a traumatic experience. But for your own sake, you really have to stop. He tortured you, and he's torturing you still. He took his own life and it wasn't your fault, Steph.'

Jess crooned gently to Steph for a few seconds, and then falteringly added, 'But Steph, that's not the whole of it. You weren't shouting out for Charlie . . . '

Steph watched her askance and Jess shook her head. 'At the end, Steph, you were shouting for Jack.'

★　★　★

'Jack, I can't go with you today,' Steph said when he called round to the hotel to pick her up, avoiding his pained expression.

He surveyed her closely. 'What's the matter? Are you ill?'

His concern only made her feel worse. She was deceiving him, lying because she didn't want to risk going away and spending the night calling out his name or Charlie's in her nightmare delirium. The night before had only succeeded in demonstrating that she wasn't ready for any of this.

'You're not scared of me, surely?' A smile tugged at the corners of his mouth as he watched her.

'No.' *More like scared of myself.*

'Are you playing hard to get, then?' His tone was teasingly humorous, but she pulled roughly away and sat on the end of the bed in a surly remonstration.

Jack sat down beside her and she stared hard at his faded jeans as he unzipped her tote bag. 'Well I guess I'll start unpacking for you, then, if you're determined you won't tell me what possible reason you could have to deter you from spending time with me.'

Jack watched her through narrowed his eyes while he continued to unpack her bag. When his hand rustled something, she looked at him sharply when she realised he was holding a rather flimsy nightdress that Jess had lent her. 'Stop it!'

He pushed his face closer to hers. 'Then, tell me what's bothering you?'

Steph sighed deeply in frustration and shrugged, unable to keep fudging or to come up with a lie that would placate Jack enough for him to relent. 'I've been talking in my sleep. It's getting worse and I can't bear to make you suffer it.'

Jack shrugged, almost laughed, but stopped himself when he saw how serious Steph was about this.

'Steph, I'm a doctor. I know how debilitating sleep disorders can be. You consistently misjudge me. If it means so much to you, I promise you'll have your own room at our destination so you needn't feel awkward. Trust me to have some sensitivity.'

Jack gently took her hand in his and kissed her fingers one by one. She gulped and the room suddenly felt too small and she was finding it hard to breathe. How on earth could she resist a man who was this effortlessly wonderful?

'Oh, Jack,' Steph wailed. 'I don't deserve it.'

'But I do.' Jack kissed her tenderly. 'Your bag's still packed. And your carriage awaits.'

★　★　★

Four hours later, after countless ruggedly tight coastal bends, they arrived at their destination. Steph knew immediately this was a far cry from Abercarrick. A twisty road had brought them to a mystery idyllic retreat — and what a haven it was!

Steph looked at Jack with mock reproach. 'You're a man with an elite taste in beaches, aren't you?'

He matched her tone by immediately raising his hands in surrender. 'What can I say? I like remote and I like the sea.'

It was the keeper's cottage of a traditional and remote lighthouse on a westerly peninsula, two hundred miles north of Abercarrick. They had traversed hair-raising roads to get there but the destination was so worth it.

The beach was indeed impressive against a heather-coloured sky. It boasted unrivalled views to the isles in pastel mauves and a total lack of any distraction whatsoever. Minimal electricity, no telephone, a small kitchen, an iron bed in each of its single rooms with patchwork bedspreads completing the scene. In essence, it was an idyll of untamed charm.

Steph didn't know what she liked more; the location or the fact that Jack hadn't assumed they'd sleep together, thus acting with gentlemanly courtesy.

He was stealing her heart a millimetre at a time. And doing so with such ease that it left her lost for words.

⋆　⋆　⋆

'On a stunning sunny day the Western Isles of Scotland can rival St Lucia for white sand, crystal waters and wild fauna — so do you like it?' Jack enquired, keen for her to share his passion for

Straness, his refuge.

He told her how whenever he wanted to flee the hurly-burly of life, this was his bolthole. It was the place he'd come to escape his woes about his brother and his wedding. But it held good memories, too — so much so that he'd bought the place.

'Seals!' Steph cried. 'Look! Real seals in that cove. Oh, I love it here.'

'Deer run wild here, too,' Jack said clearly pleased with the fruition of his plan, a smile spreading over his features. 'Now that really is something to see.'

Steph breathed, 'I've always loved watching seals.'

'Wait until you see the bats at dusk.'

They sipped on elderflower wine and sparkling water and admired the views, savoured the scent of the sweetly perfumed roses on the table, and gave in to the urges they'd held in check for so long and kissed frequently.

Savouring his smell, and gasping at his touch, Steph finally murmured,

'Jack. Let's go and choose which bedroom you want.' But she knew she wouldn't let him sleep alone tonight. Not after bringing her here and making her fall hook, line and sinker in love with him.

16

Steph awoke feeling confused and disorientated and then immediately became aware that she was lying in Jack's warm, reassuring embrace. His body was firm, strong and immensely comforting.

She became wholly conscious of the fact that they'd spent the night together ... same room, same intent. No regrets.

But now she had no time to savour the feeling or get used to it; there was an insistent rapping noise from somewhere — she guessed the door. Steph moved from the magnetising heat of Jack's body, sleepy and fumbling, and scrambled into clothes.

Jack roused and pushed a hand over his sleepy face. 'What's up? Where are you off to?'

'Going to get the door ... ' she

murmured. 'Who can it be? No one knows we're here.'

His iron grasp pulled her back and stopped her in her tracks, his voice holding a forceful edge.

'No, Steph. It could be anyone. I'll go and see to it.'

She couldn't miss the tense clenching of his jaw as he moved away and watched him dress quickly as the noise continued, growing ever louder. It was only then that she looked at her watch: ten past midnight. Jack slipped out quickly, his absence making her realise she was suddenly cold and shivering.

Who on earth could be at the door at this time? And what could they want from a couple in a remote coastal cottage? Unless something was wrong. Something at Glen Muir? Her thoughts immediately jumped to Ally and her baby.

Don't think the worst, Steph, she schooled herself.

But her pulse was already revving and a heavy lump of lead had settled in her stomach. Something was wrong; she knew it before Jack even returned to her side.

★　★　★

Jack cursed softly under his breath when he finally returned to the cottage. His romantic getaway with Steph had gone from heaven to hell in a matter of hours.

Willie Anderson, the messenger from the nearest cottage a mile away, had been less than impressed with Jess's orders to go and get her boss. The cottage's remote nature and patchy mobile reception meant she hadn't been able to get through, and Willie had kindly let Jack go and use his own house phone.

He'd actually wished he hadn't.

The news wasn't good and would mean an immediate return in the morning. No way was he forcing Steph to dress so that they could drive through the night.

Steph greeted him, pale-faced and worried, at the door as soon as he returned.

So much for an idyllic break with the woman he was so swiftly falling for. Time alone; escape. But then again, Glen Muir had always had an iron hold over his life. It always would; sometimes in a good way. Sometimes — like now — less so.

'We'll have to go back at daylight. Jess has summoned us. Ally's gone into labour, so Fraser's at the hospital and there's been other developments. I'm sorry it's wrecked our escape.'

'Is Ally okay?'

'Fine. I'd guess by the time we get back she may have had the baby. Jess was still waiting for news and she's frantic.'

'Is she worried, then? Are there complications?'

Steph shoved her hand through her bed-tousled hair and Jack thought she looked so adorable — like a little girl lost. All he wanted to do was lock the

264

door behind him and crush her against him, losing all memory of reality in a bone-melting kiss.

But that couldn't be.

'You're not to worry, Ally will be fine, but there have been other developments at Glen Muir . . . '

Steph was watching him, waiting for more. As much as it pained him to admit it, he had to tell her why the rush back was urgent when they could be of no help to Ally or Fraser during the birth of their baby.

'It's Hamish. He's back. And he's in the mood for war.'

*   *   *

Steph was sad to leave the lighthouse at Straness. The peace, tranquillity and romantic seclusion had been blissful, if surreal. Things would hardly be likely to remain so on their return to Glen Muir.

She'd sighed as they shut the door behind them and tried to commit every detail to memory. In her mind's eye that lowly keeper's cottage would always be precious. Even if it had all ended too abruptly; they left just after six and covered the miles back to Abercarrick swiftly.

Jack pulled up outside a small shop just after nine. It seemed to be in the middle of nowhere, though a tiny railway station stood surrounded by rolling hills and glen. There was not a lot else, she noted, as Jack unclipped his seat belt and opened the door. The shop seemed to be an outlet for tourist crafts.

'I'm going in here; anything you need?'

Steph shook her head, but was pleased of a chance to stretch her legs. She enjoyed the brief pleasure of watching Jack run lithely towards the shop.

Scotland was growing on her. The vast desolation and sombre charm of the countryside. She wondered where such an isolated train station took its passengers?

Jack returned and pushed a small,

silk bag into her hand.

'What's this?'

'Open it,' he instructed as she peered tentatively inside.

Steph found her heart was thudding — she held her breath as she carefully removed the contents and held it up to examine it; a gemstone, oblong-shaped, flat and smooth; a stone hued in the palest lilac that could almost have been designed to lay flat in the centre of the palm of her hand, cool but strangely comforting.

'It's beautiful, but what is it?' she asked intrigued and ran her fingers on its smoothness.

'It's a talisman,' Jack said simply. 'And a reminder of our stay. My sister is a great believer in crystals. That's an amethyst and some think their healing powers are mumbo-jumbo, but Marnie's a convert.'

'Thank you.' Steph turned it over and over, admiring its lustre. 'It's beautiful.'

'It's also renowned for its restorative powers.'

'What for?

'It eases recurring nightmares.'

Steph looked up at him, bowled over. 'Thank you.'

'I care deeply about you, you know,' he said quietly. 'It's a protecting crystal, from me to you.'

Steph gently kissed his cheek, savouring the now familiar Jack smell, her heart swelling as she wished they'd had just another day to savour.

'I feel cherished,' she confided.

'And I'll keep cherishing you for as long as you'll let me.'

* * *

'Am I breaking up a party?' Jack asked on their return to Glen Muir. He'd walked into his office and come face to face with the brother he hadn't seen since he ran off with the woman he'd thought he loved.

Steph looked on as Jack looked at Hamish disparagingly, then pointedly stared at the open decanter of whisky and the glasses on the desk.

'Helping yourself to the good stuff already? Some things don't change,' Jack remarked. 'I'll make sure you're billed for it later, never fear.'

'Nice welcome,' said Hamish in a Scottish brogue that had elements of his life in Australia thrown in. 'Don't worry. I'll note it all down. You always were a bit OCD around the edges, Jack. Can't you diagnose an immediate need to calm down, and write a prescription for yourself?'

Jack looked tall and dark and had a frightening fire in his eyes that Steph had never seen before. It would have put her on edge had she not been shocked enough.

Hamish was taller and more muscular than Jack; broader, with close-cropped hair and a deep, dark tan.

'So, Jack, how's tricks?' he asked and stood up from behind his brother's desk.

Steph felt it was a definite liberty to go and sit in someone's private workspace, given that Hamish had been so long off the scene. It didn't augur well. Clearly Hamish McGregor liked to assert his dominance and didn't hesitate to think about the feelings of others.

It was only then that Steph noticed the dark-haired woman sitting with her back to the door. She turned to reveal herself to be the much-hyped Paula.

Steph drew in a sharp breath of surprise. The woman was truly beautiful. Steph could see why Jack had been so in love — pale skin, violet eyes, dark brows so perfect she could have been a shop window china doll.

Except for the visibly pregnant tummy, outlined in a clingy maternity top. Paula looked to be pretty far gone and Steph would have guessed her to be seven months or so.

'Sorry we couldn't give you any warning, Jack,' Paula added, making her presence felt for the first time. 'I had to attend to baby matters and we flew before we had a chance to warn you.'

'You're pretty good at doing things your way and not thinking of the consequences until later,' Jack replied, gruffly adding, 'Couldn't — or wouldn't? You always did prefer the element of surprise, didn't you?'

Steph stood back, sensing that this was no place for her — this was a family dispute that had to be aired and she really needed to let them have their space to do it in.

She briefly touched Jack's hand. 'I'll be in my room if you need me.'

'Aren't you going to introduce us?' Paula asked. Her accent was as polished as her image, but there was a sharp steel behind those perfect violet eyes that put Steph immediately on alert. Her smile was saccharine-sweet but there was nothing soft about her.

'This is Steph. My girlfriend,' Jack said. Turning to Steph he added more softly, 'I'll see you later; you should get some rest.'

'Had a wild weekend? Didn't disturb you, did we?' Paula added as Steph turned to leave the room.

Until that point Steph had felt like an intruder, a bystander. She had no interest in involving herself in Jack's family get-together, other than to offer her support and comfort. It wasn't her place. But the ice-laden comment made her turn.

'Yeah, you know Jack . . . so romantic, loads of stamina. What woman wouldn't fall for a weekend away with a man like him? Only a crazy woman would walk away.'

Paula's open-eyed shock was well worth the interjection and its attendant increase in pulse-rate. Steph wanted to punch the air in triumph.

She gave Jack a sidelong smile and then left them to it.

Inside she was willing Jack to give them both barrels without reservation — it was Hamish and Paula's day of reckoning and recompense was long overdue.

★   ★   ★

An hour passed. Then an hour-and-a-half. Steph showered but she couldn't nap, even though she was so tired. She was longing for news of Ally, as well as feeling almost desperate to hear from Jack, too.

Eventually, tiring of waiting and pacing, she went down to reception to check if Fraser had called in with news — but she drew a blank, which only succeeded in worrying her more.

Feeling suffocated by her own swirling thoughts, she was about to go outside when a voice drew her up sharp. It was Jess.

'Come and see these,' Jess urged. 'In the library.'

'Hi, how are you? How did you handle the mini-crisis of Hamish arriving out of the blue?' Steph asked, eager to discuss the recent events with her new friend.

'With sarcasm and a singularly unhelpful manner, actually!' Jess replied. 'He's a weasel, that one. How dare he come back here acting like Lord Mighty.

Typical that Jack wasn't here.'

'He's with him now,' Steph told her. 'With Paula as well. I left them to talk it out — or rather, shout it out — in private.'

Steph followed Jess into the hotel's expansive panelled library. It was a popular room with guests who wanted some quiet time, but today it was empty.

Steph gasped when she saw what was awaiting her there.

'Are these okay?' Jess asked. She was blushing and twiddling the wedding ring on her finger.

Steph examined the large mounted photographs featuring Jess and Gordon dressed up in wedding finery. There were additional pictures of them with the children and a series of informal pictures of them in casual dress, too. But some of the shots — the ones of just the two of them — out on the hotel terrace and by the loch were simply stunning.

Steph opened her eyes wide with

delight. 'You certainly pulled out the stops, didn't you?'

Jess hugged her warmly. 'This place is like family to me. I'll do whatever is needed to support it. You said you needed them quickly, so I saw no reason to hang about.'

Steph hugged her back, knowing Glen Muir Castle Hotel had its staunchest advocate in Jess Cameron. 'You're an absolute wonder, Jess.'

A light tapping on the door made them both turn from their mutual embrace. The receptionist, Katie was standing with a broad smile on her face.

'It's a boy!' she announced excitedly. 'They're naming him Lewis Brodie Munro. Eight pounds, nine ounces, and mother and baby are both just dandy!'

Jess squealed happily and Steph grinned with relief.

At least something had gone right today. Steph ardently hoped that Jack's predicament would soon be sorted too.

17

Steph wanted to head off for a walk around the lochside, but as she stepped out into the grounds she quickly revised the plan when she heard voices speaking in soft tones.

And one of them was most definitely Jack's. She didn't want to snoop, but there was something in his tone that alarmed her.

There was clearly no arguing going on and the conversation was most definitely between a man and a woman — a woman she could only assume was Paula.

'You're looking well, Jack,' said the woman's voice.

'I am well. Overworked, but I'm enjoying what I do. Dad's a big concern to me, though.'

'How is he?'

'The dementia is definitely worsening. You must make Hamish go and visit him, now that you're back.'

'Hamish won't go,' the woman confided in a voice that clearly indicated that it was a closed topic. 'You know Hamish. He's guilty. Guilty that he went off without word, guilty about you, guilty about his duplicity and desertion. It hasn't all been plain sailing for us, Jack.'

'Sorry if I don't sound too sympathetic. I've had rather a lot on my plate at this end, too,' Jack replied drily.

Steph began to move off, telling herself she had no business eavesdropping and that Jack would tell her all about it when he was ready to — but then the next sentence caused her to stop in her tracks . . .

'You know you're kidding yourself with this Steph woman, Jack. You don't fool me, you never could. She's nothing to you.'

'And since when did you know me so completely?' Jack responded swiftly.

Steph took a sharp intake of breath and her hand flew to her mouth to stifle the sound. What on earth made Paula

Banning view herself as a fit person pass judgement on Steph's relationship with Jack?

'Oh, I know more than you realise, Jack. I loved you once and in many ways I still do, you know. I wonder if you've you ever really stopped loving me?'

There was a pause.

It was a long and ominous pause during which Steph could hear her heart thud in her ears. She didn't dare even breathe for fear of giving herself away. She closed her eyes, willing the silence to break, willing the man she loved to say something to put the spiteful, jealous, controlling woman back in her place.

Yet she was just as fearful as could be of what she might learn in the next heartbeat.

'Steph is a girl with a bright smile and a warm heart . . . ' he answered falteringly.

Steph's heart pounded and she stood statue still.

'But you didn't answer my question,' Paula persisted. 'Do you love me still?

Did you get over me?'

Jack's voice was unmistakable, his tone slow and spent when he replied, 'How could I ever get over you, Paula? You were all I ever wanted.'

★　★　★

Steph decided to use the key Jack had given her to leave the hotel by the back exit. She still couldn't think straight or focus. It felt as if she'd downed a bottle of whisky without even a pause for breath.

The conversation kept going round in her head. Jack still loved Paula. He'd admitted it. He couldn't see past her lies.

They'd been sitting outside, talking about old times in hushed voices, acting like reunited lovers — and after all the woman had put him through! Was he crazy?

Anger mixed with despair bubbled slowly inside her and rose, clouding her thoughts.

If this was really how Jack McGregor viewed things — if he'd been sidling up to her as second best — then perhaps he truly deserved Paula, after all. They deserved each other.

To think that she'd listened to him, had believed and cared, that she had begun to love him with everything she had. She had allowed Jack into her heart, to slowly thaw out that frozen-over, chilled area of her emotions — only for him to break it now. What a fool she'd been!

Turning back, she vowed to go and pack and leave immediately. There was no way she'd hang around Glen Muir, kidding herself and believing Jack's lies.

Did he view romancing her as a cheap route to marketing? Advice on the side from a woman who'd fallen for a few tired lines and romantic gestures?

Steph went indoors, feeling resolute; she was leaving, and no one was going to change her mind.

★ ★ ★

Passing by the library, Steph's luck completely bottomed out when she ran into the woman who'd caused all the fuss.

A tiny voice inside her head reminded Steph that she should be thanking Paula; she'd opened her eyes to the full extent of Jack's duplicity. Yet somehow she couldn't bring herself to feel anything positive for a woman who had schemed and demanded and controlled in the way she had done.

'Ah, just the person,' Paula almost purred. 'Could you rustle me up a herbal tea? I'm parched. Chamomile preferably, though I'll take whatever this Godforsaken hole can offer.'

While outrage simmered and Steph itched to tell her to fetch it herself as she wasn't working, something made her comply. Why dump the task on someone else when it may give her a chance to get in a few choice words of her own?

Swiftly she made the tea and took it to the library where Paula was reclining on one of the big sofas, surrounded by fashion magazines and a plethora of high-maintenance aids, from air spritzers to eye masks.

'Your tea,' Steph said stiffly, making sure the china cup chinked in its saucer to disturb her. 'And just for the record, I know what you're doing and why you're back. Jack told me while we were away together about his father and the new power of attorney. You're here to stake a claim. You think the dust will have settled and now you can make a mercenary move.'

Paula stared at Steph as if she were a guttersnipe upstart. One beautifully groomed brow slowly raised in disdain. 'And what exactly does it have to do with you?'

Steph forced herself taller and determined not to feel inferior or thwarted just because this woman was as polished as a brass plaque. 'I happen to care about Jack — and I care about the hotel and its people too. And I can't stand to see your falsehoods, masquerading to secure a foothold in Glen Muir. I happen to think your motivations are financial and I'll not be swayed in my views, even if you have Jack fooled.'

Paula motioned to the swell of her blooming tummy. 'I'm pregnant, darling. Daddy will give me money now that he's seen me with child, so why would I care about Glen Muir? I admit that Hamish has this crazy idea about settling here to have the baby, but I could never really come back to this dreary-place.'

Steph scoffed, incredulous at Paula's confession. 'You'd have a child as a capital investment opportunity? I knew you were low but I didn't realise how far you'd go.'

'Oh, don't judge, sweetie. You're in love with a guy who can't love you back — hardly the moral high ground credentials. In fact, I'd say you're pretty pathetic.'

Paula's sneer was the most genuine thing she'd seen from the woman since they'd met.

'He loves me like an addiction, you

see,' Paula went on, well into her stride now. 'And if I have my way we'll get Hamish's inheritance back. Jack will realise he's gone too far and all will be well again. You can't really hope to compete with me, darling, though you're welcome to stick around and try. I do enjoy a bit of competition, even if it is pretty weak.'

Paula could throw all the verbal daggers she wanted; Steph wouldn't stoop to answer back.

Sadly, addiction was the thing that had ruined her life before — and if Jack truly felt that way about Paula, she pitied him. The woman didn't deserve a moment of his time.

Paula stroked her bump and leaned over to sip her tea.

Steph found herself regretting that she'd given her such satisfaction and fed her ego even more fully.

'On second thoughts, perhaps it's best if you do go, for all concerned. You'd always just be second best,' Paula added.

If Charlie had taught her anything, it was that an exit in dignified silence was the only possible winning move. Steph walked away and didn't argue. She already felt second best.

And that was something she had long ago vowed she'd never stand for again.

★ ★ ★

Just when she thought she was getting somewhere, the one man she really didn't want to see came out and caught her in the act of loading up her car.

'Steph, what's happening? You're going somewhere? Has something happened?' Jack asked, looking concerned and as if nothing at all untoward had happened.

'I'm going to see Ally,' she lied. 'I'll be back soon.'

Jack came to her and slid his arms around her waist. Inside she was trembling and ready to either shout or cry at the impact those strong, caring arms had on her roiling emotions.

She bit her lip as she asked, 'And how are things with your family now?' As if she didn't know the answer!

'Hardly ideal. I've told them to go,' he replied. 'They've no business coming back here and I've told them that I have nothing more to say to them.'

She wished she hadn't lied, she wished he hadn't come and hugged her — and oh, how she wished she didn't know the awful truth of what Jack really felt. She decided there and then that there was no going back — she had to tell him that she knew.

'I'm lying,' she said with a deep sigh. 'I'm leaving for good.'

Jack stared at her as if she'd just told him some terrible, incomprehensible news. Instead of arguing she merely bent down to pick up another bag to stow in the boot.

'What?'

'You heard me, Jack. I'm leaving Glen Muir. Let's just say I've only just realised how flimsy your lines have been and how powerful Paula Banning's hold over you still is.'

'Paula? You're joking, right?'

'I heard you both.'

'When?'

'Earlier, when you were talking outside on the terrace.'

Jack bit back a retort and stayed silent.

She forced the words out in spite of the pain behind them. 'You said I was just a girl with a bright smile and a warm heart.'

Jack's tone grew terse. 'And you didn't stay to hear me finish the sentence.'

'I don't want to. I've heard enough.'

'Yes, a bright smile and a warm heart — and a woman I love more than I ever dreamed was possible when I was with her. A woman who's turned my life around for the better and opened my eyes to true worth.'

'I heard you telling her how you're still in love with her. Only now that means you've a crush on your brother's pregnant wife. While I'd love to stay and see how the dramatic soap of Glen Muir pans out, frankly I'd rather miss the cliff-hanger.'

Jack pushed his hand through his hair and let out a long, low breath. 'You clearly don't believe me, but I'm telling you truthfully that you've got it wrong, Steph. I'm not still in love with Paula.'

'I heard you tell her!'

'All I was saying is that I'd never get over her completely because she left me bitter, hurt and angry.'

'Nice try, Jack. But I've believed your honeyed lines for way too long.' Steph's hurt at what she thought was his betrayal showed in her tone.

'It's the truth, Steph. Truly! I was a car wreck at her hands and I told her that to her face today. She left me duped and torn and fit for nothing but self-doubt and, if I'm honest, self-loathing as well as hatred of my brother. I could never love her, nor ever respect her, again — how could you think that I could? As for Hamish, well, I pity him if you want to know. He's got himself in a fix with money and he's only back here to see what he can get out of Glen Muir. I gave him my answer — nothing. The pair of them aren't welcome here any more.'

Lies, Steph thought irrationally. *He's covering his tracks. Just like Charlie did.*

She marched over the gravel like a squaddie on a mission. 'It's too late. I don't want to hear.'

'And this is how much I mean to you? You won't even give me a chance?' Jack defended himself and accused her simultaneously in his desperation to make her stay.

'You're still in love with Paula, and you have more than enough pulls on your time without adding me to the mix.'

'Isn't that for me to decide? As for Paula — you really can't be serious, Steph.'

He was watching her with dark glittering eyes; eyes that she'd previously thought shone like a star-filled sky. Eyes that, it now seemed, hid the real truth of his heart.

'You're in denial, Jack. You have a lot of things to come to terms with and I don't need this in my life. You need time to unravel your issues.'

'I don't want time. I want you.'

She fished out the envelope that she'd earlier shoved into her pocket and thrust it at him. It was a letter to Jess, the only one person at Glen Muir that she felt was owed explanations for her hasty departure.

'I don't want to be involved in this family feud of yours. Can you give this to Jess, please?'

'Another way of saying you want out? And you give Jess more courtesy than you give to me. Please, Steph . . . '

'I need to get back to my real life now. Let's not pretend it was ever going to be different for either of us. Keep the money for the hotel — I know you need it and I want you to have it.'

Jack's jaw twitched with supressed anger and despair. 'Then if that's how you feel, I guess there's nothing more to say,' he answered and turned and walked away, holding her crumpled envelope in his clenched, determined fist.

18

Steph had packed at full speed and hadn't even bothered to check out. She'd call Ally and Fraser later to explain. Right now she didn't need to revisit things — she just wanted out. But she had only driven as far as the main B-road to Darrochinch when she realised there was a car tailing her.

Closer inspection made her groan as she realised she'd have to pull in. It was Jess, in hot pursuit like something from a bad cop movie. Finding a lay-by and knowing an interrogation would inevitably follow suit, she pulled in, prepared to be firm and strong. She was leaving and she wasn't coming back.

Jess called out to her as she pulled in behind her, 'And where do you think you're going?'

'Away,' Steph answered, trying not to

make eye contact. 'Read the note I left you.'

'I already did, Steph, but I truly don't understand the lunacy of this escapade of yours.'

'It's not lunacy. Three words — Jack and Paula.'

'You're joking, surely?' Jess scoffed openly when she reached her. 'Have you lost your marbles?'

'Yes, I have — I was crazy to have listened to Jack's lines in the first place. He loves her, probably always has and always will. I hope the three of them will be happy together, however they choose to sort their mess out.'

'They won't be sorting out anything. The two usurpers are leaving, pronto, thanks to a little direct interference from yours truly,' Jess announced proudly. It was clear she was feeling rather good about whatever she'd done.

'What? I don't understand.'

'I told Paula and Hamish a few home truths. Like how I may know too much about local gossip, but sometimes that can turn out to be a good thing, to be in the know.'

Jess stepped closer to Steph and linked her arm into hers and continued, 'You see I just happened to mention to Paula and Hamish that I knew she'd had a fling before him. We had a famous golfer staying nearby a while back. He was training for a championship tournament and staying in a wing of the golf club. Paula was all over him like a rash — and she was still seeing Jack then. I thought Hamish should know he wasn't her first hot pursuit.'

Steph watched her friend. 'And how did that go down?'

'Like fireworks!' Jess crowed. 'They're probably still yelling at each other yet!'

'I'm not coming back, Jess. Wild horses and all that. The McGregors need to find their own way out of the quagmire.'

'Steph, don't be stupid enough to believe that woman; she's a liar through and through.'

'And Jack is pure as the driven snow, right?'

'What makes you doubt him?'

'Let's say I have my reasons. I'm not convinced he's not still in love with her.'

'What rubbish!' Jess refuted, her eyes aglow.

'Is it?'

'Hamish wasn't her love at first sight as much as she likes to pretend. He was her second in line. She would've preferred a wealthy, famous golfer — if he'd been sufficiently interested in her, that is. She just likes the chase and the conquest; it massages her own ego. Can't you see that, Steph?'

'It's really none of my business.'

'So you'll walk away from the best thing that ever happened to you simply because of something you overheard a spiteful woman like Paula saying?'

'I have a life, Jess and it's time I got back to it and focused on rebuilding it. Ally and Fraser will understand.'

'And what about Jack? How do you expect him to understand? You're prepared to just walk out on him after what he's been through?'

Steph shook her head. Just thinking about him and saying his name hurt her deeply. She did love him, heart and soul, and she had to admit that, but she couldn't risk losing her self-respect in pursuing that love.

'Jack and I are over, Jess. Perhaps we never even really got started. Maybe it was just wishful thinking on my part.'

'You're wrong, Steph, I know it. Jack loves you.' Jess shook her head despairingly. 'He *needs* you.'

'I need space. It's just all too much, too soon and I have emotional baggage of my own.'

'And letting some waster who didn't deserve you — and freaked you out with his risky ways — get in the way of something as wonderful as you and Jack is just letting one disaster compound another,' Jess said firmly, determined not to let her friend throw her life away.

There was a lump lodged in Steph's throat the size of a rainforest-dwelling amphibian, but she pushed through in spite of it. 'It's too late, I'm going. I really do need to work out my future. For what it's worth I've invested money in Glen Muir and I won't be withdrawing it. I still believe in the hotel's potential and in my friends, Jess. But for now I just need to be allowed to go and work out whether I still believe in myself.'

'Jack needs you . . . '

'No, Jess. Jack needs to untangle his own heart.'

'Stop deluding yourself, Steph. You and I both know you're madly in love with Jack. It's there glowing stark and clear in your eyes. Why on earth can't you just open up your heart and admit. it? Does he even know how you really feel about him?'

'I do love him, but it makes no difference now. I can't trust in us any more. All we had was a brief fling and that's not enough for me to up sticks and change my whole life for.'

'Then you're making a big mistake. You'll realise it one day.'

Jess turned to leave. Steph put her hand on her arm to stop her, holding back the tears for all that she was worth.

'You're right about me loving Jack,' she told Jess. 'And I'll miss you all more than you'll know. This is breaking my heart, but going is just something I have to do, Jess — please try to understand. And, Jess . . . ' she hesitated. 'Please don't tell Jack what I told you about my feelings for him.'

'If you really want me not to, then of course I would never betray a confidence. But you're doing the wrong thing, Steph. As for Jack, he deserves a hellcat to stick up for him so he's got me whether he wants me or not.'

Jess moved towards her car, then paused and looked back at Steph. 'I may eventually forgive you for walking out on him. But you're wrong, Steph. You'll realise it too late some day, but you're wrong, I know you are.'

★　★　★

Jack McGregor was moping; a sad and solitary figure in a rowing boat, out on an inky-black loch, nursing a heavy heart and a busy mind.

He hadn't gone on the loch since his teens, when he used to fish for trout well past dusk.

Tonight he was skimming stones in a haze of self-pity. He managed a few passable attempts but the maximum he could achieve was three bounces on the loch's murky surface.

Alas, wasn't that the case with most things in his life? Apart from the business, which ironically was now on something of a high. But nothing was right without her. How could it ever be?

Jack selected a smooth, flat stone from his collection at the bottom of the boat. Its similarity to the shape of the amethyst he'd given Steph struck him, and that only served to make him feel even worse.

Had the crystal worked? He hadn't had the good fortune to spend another night with her to find out, and now

299

he'd never know now.

'Hey!' shouted Jess from the shoreline, cupping her mouth with her hands. She had Phoenix beside her. 'Get yourself over here, McGregor!'

He threw the stone. It hit the water and sank without trace.

Jess continued, 'Get back here, now!'

Jack lurched precariously over to the other side of the boat. The craft wobbled, water lapping into the sides, but he made it to the bench and rowed to the shore in a few easy strokes.

'Can't a man have any peace around here?'

'Not when you're in depressed mode. Whether you want company or not, it's what you're about to get.'

Jack scowled, let out a groan and swept his wet hair away from his face; a face that he hadn't shaved in a few days now because he couldn't summon up enough interest.

'And you'd better shave before you go and see her.'

'What are you talking about?'

The crickets chirruped nearby and night sounds floated towards them; an insistent bird, an owl, a bat. Jack had already watched the bats fly over the loch, highlighted by the setting sun, and an amazing sight when in flight at dusk.

Magical, Steph had called the spectacle when they'd watched it together. He could recall her voice easily, even smell her, as if she were really there by his side.

'You need to pack up your pride, go and see her, and bring her back here,' Jess told him emphatically.

Jack looked at her with derision. 'Why should I, when she thinks so little of me?'

'Because you love her and you'll lose her if you don't.'

'It was her decision to leave.'

'Because she's had her trust shattered, and along came Paula Banning and compounded that by feeding her lies about the man she's crazy about. She doesn't doubt you, Jack — she doubts herself. Go and make her listen.'

'She won't answer my calls.' None of his repeated phone calls or messages had been returned and it seemed Steph was giving him a clear message to leave her alone.

'And that's enough for you? She doesn't answer your calls so you throw in the towel?' Jess asked. 'You need her — you know it and I know it — and if you don't go and get her, you'll lose the best thing you've ever had.'

Jess patted Phoenix, who lay down by her side and looked up as if agreeing with her mistress's words. 'From where I'm standing, all I saw was a woman utterly in love with you and just dying to have it reciprocated.' Her words hung in the air.

'Really?' Jack asked.

'Really. You love her, don't you?'

'Yes, I love her, Jess, but she made it perfectly clear that she doesn't want me. She doesn't even believe me.'

'And wasn't it the same with you? Crossed wires and past hurts messing up the transmission,' Jess said firmly.

'You have to let go of your emotional baggage every bit as much as Steph does. You have to make her believe you, but to do that you have to believe in yourself. Just believe that she loves you, Jack, and the rest will follow.'

★   ★   ★

'Mum, take it easy,' Steph called from her recliner deckchair in their Abergavenny garden. She was surrounded by the Sunday newspapers, and had been back from Scotland for a week. She'd taken extra care not to chance upon any of the Glen Muir hotel ads in the supplements, though she knew they would be there. It really wasn't her problem any more.

'Come and have some tea, Mum.'

The sun was baking hot and Steph wore her denim cut-offs and a deep purple spaghetti strap sun top, with the desired result that she was bronzing nicely.

Her inner turmoil was unresolved,

but she reasoned she could hide it better with a good suntan on her limbs.

'You sure you don't want to call those people in Scotland again, let them know how you are? Won't they be missing you?' her mother asked in a concerned tone.

'No,' Steph answered swiftly. 'I've already spoken to Jess.'

'I'd have thought they'd still need your help. Didn't Ally need you as a worker for a while, what with the new baby and all? I know you had planned on staying.' When it came to pushing and making her point, Glenda was a master. Besides, she knew there was something not quite right with her daughter and she was determined to get to the bottom of it.

'They'll manage.' Steph didn't even look up from her reading.

'You'll want to go back soon, I should think,' Glenda said, pricking her finger with her sewing needle. 'You know, I can manage here without you and you don't have to nursemaid the shop. Or you could go to London and start finding a new job?' Glenda sucked the wound.

Serves her right, thought Steph savagely. 'No plans, I fancy hanging around here for a while,' she said firmly. 'So I'm afraid you're stuck with me. I'm hurt that you're so keen to see the back of your daughter. I'd have thought you'd be delighted to have me keep you company,' she added with mock indignation.

Glenda gave her daughter a sharp tut of irritation.

'Tea,' Steph reiterated, pouring a fresh cup and adding milk.

'That would be nice.' The distinctive voice came from a stunning blonde in wraparound glasses and a knee-skimming, show-stopping pink shirt dress. Marnie McGregor was leaning on the garden gate, as if she'd just happened down a country lane and found them.

Steph stared over the top of her mug. 'Marnie!'

'Don't you answer your door? Been

ringing that bell for ages.' Steph jumped up and went to hug her. 'You're browner than when I last saw you,' Marnie said. 'Obviously your mum's letting you sit idle instead of enlisting you for garden muscle.'

'Why are you here and why didn't you say you were coming?' Steph led her to the patio. Seeing her mother was clearly intrigued, she did the necessary introductions.

'Jess tracked you down Columbo-style,' Marnie confessed. 'It took some doing — especially getting Glenda to agree to keep quiet until I got here!'

Steph stared at her mother, who had the decency to blush.

'I'd have phoned you first,' Marnie explained, 'but I fancied making it a surprise.'

'How are you?' Steph asked. She could detect a certain hard-nosed, I-mean-business-and-intend-to-get-some-answers demeanour underneath Marnie's chit-chat. She hadn't believed the surprise unannounced arrival for a minute.

Since her mother was now hovering over them with ears like radar, Steph made a suggestion. 'Fancy a walk? It's too beautiful a day to waste.' She gave Marnie a wink and dragged her away.

They walked side by side, Marnie looking as if she'd stepped from the pages of a glossy magazine and Steph feeling like a waif in denim rags.

Distant appreciative clapping drifted towards them from the nearby ground where some lads were playing rugby. Steph observed male eyes following their sedate walk.

'So you're on your way back to Abercarrick?' Steph ventured.

'We can go back together,' Marnie said adamantly. 'I can book into a B and B here and wait until you're ready, of course.'

Steph let a few seconds pass before she answered. 'I'm not going back, Marnie.'

'Oh, yes you are!' Marnie returned, looking incensed.

'Things won't be the same again and

Jack knows my feelings plainly.' Steph tried to defend her stance.

Marnie simply gave a disbelieving snort. 'So why exactly are you hiding here, acting like an idiot when my brother is going crazy without you?'

'He's going crazy?' Why did it feel so good to know that? 'So he and Paula have resolved their differences, then?' she added bitterly. 'It's all happy families now?'

'Hardly. Hamish and Paula have gone back to Australia, and nothing's changed — except you've gone and suddenly Jack isn't even shaving or listening to anything anyone says to him. His brain's gone AWOL. I suspect it's followed his heart into hiding. He's a mess without you.'

It had been two days since the messages from Jack had stopped. Steph had been watching the phone and her policy to leave the messages unreturned had eventually worked as desired; he was finally leaving her alone.

Didn't he see it was for his own

good? Didn't he realise she had to stay strong, to give him the space he needed?

'Paula's gone. Jess told me to come here and talk some sense into you. How can you be so blind? Jack loves you.' Marnie's sapphire blue eyes clearly showed how fiercely protective she was of her brother.

'He still has issues to resolve from his past. He never got over Paula in the first place.'

Steph's heart was beating fast and she could feel fireworks slowly start to ignite inside her, shooting into the air in a frenzied display of dawning hope.

'Steph, Jack is under no illusions. Paula saw him as a Scottish ancestral meal ticket because of Dad's historic legacy. When she found out he struggled with crippling estate debts for years she soon showed her mettle. She kept pushing Jack to persuade Dad to sell; she made no bones about her dissatisfaction. Her dreams of a Scottish pile to play lady of the manor in were dashed.

But when Hamish came home with a big retirement pension, strapping muscles and enough savings to keep her entertained and interested, she found a new direction. Jack's no fool, Steph; he sees her for what she really is.'

Steph stared at her, raising her hand to her mouth. *He told me and I didn't believe him!* she suddenly realised. Why hadn't Jack told her all of this properly? She sighed and stuck her hands in her shorts pockets, her thoughts swimming.

'She told me Jack would always want her and, like a fool, I believed it . . . '

Marnie squeezed her arm in reassurance. 'Paula always was a consummate actress — maybe now you'll see why Jack is better off without her. But it doesn't alter the fact that she's gone and left him again — and now so have you . . . '

Steph felt her pulse race and it made her feel overwhelmed.

'You and Jack love each other,' Marnie declared. 'It's utterly plain to everyone who sees you together. He only wants you for who you are, Steph.' She paused and tipped her head to look directly into Steph's eyes. 'And from the look on your face, it's reciprocated . . . why can't you just let yourself love him? Why won't you tell him?'

'It's just that . . . ' Steph stumbled for the words. 'I suppose I'm . . . I'm scared of loving someone and being let down . . . like before . . . scared of hurting that much again!' Tears trickled down her face unchecked now, as she abandoned her attempts to hold back the tide of emotions surging through her.

Marnie paused and gave her a sisterly hug. 'Oh, Steph . . . Jack would never hurt you. Don't you know that? Come back with me, Steph, you know it's where you belong. Come home to Glen Muir.'

19

Steph's knitting was defeating her and the sheep by the shop door was silently goading her about it. Tossing her needles aside, she vowed to take it back and start again. Later.

Emlyn the sheep sat by the door, unimpressed by Steph's mood. Its rotund belly, amiable smile and jaunty knitting needles were supposed to be endearing. Steph hated that plastic sheep; her mother loved it like a prized antique and it had become the shop's quirky mascot. Emlyn was an intrinsic part of Baxter's Wools but that didn't give it a licence to annoy her.

Yet here she was, back in Abergavenny with the familiar racks of multifarious, multi-coloured yarns stacked to the rafters. Steph still hadn't been able to muster the courage to call Jack and Abercarrick, Scotland, was just a place she was trying really hard not to remember.

Steph sniffed and contemplated moving Emlyn into the store room, but wouldn't it just win if she did? Sometimes you had to show forbearance and turn a blind eye — or so she'd preached to Jack.

It hurt to recall her words.

Trade that morning had hardly been brisk, but at least she had work, a roof over her head — and hiding out in Wales was way better than returning to London to face the crossroads conundrum of her future.

It was amazing how much more slowly a slow day could go when there was no company. She missed Jess's jokes; she missed Ally and wondered how the baby was doing. She missed looking out at mountains and lochs, missed the hustle and bustle of the hotel work. She even missed Roger the cockerel.

She flicked through a magazine, none of the pages registering, then turned up the radio and tried not to think about her current lack of finances. Her building society account was barren, overdraft loomed and she couldn't even afford a latte. As she reached for the biscuit tin, she said a silent prayer of thanks for chocolate shortbread as her consolation.

The door's tinkly bells brought the promise of a customer and Steph looked up with a smile that faded fast on her lips.

'Hello.'

It was Jack. He was in a dinner suit as if he was on his way to Cannes, looking taller and more arresting than she remembered, framed by the small doorway.

Her brain couldn't compute Jack suddenly being here, standing there right in front of her. It seemed surreal; he didn't belong somehow.

But, Lord, he did look wonderful . . . his glossy, touchable dark hair, that quizzical stare and amazing profile. And dressed just as he had been the first time they'd met, she realised with a start. It hurt just to look at him.

'Hello,' she said, struggling to hold her emotions in check.

'I'm in need of your help,' he answered.

'Looking for wool? You're a bit overdressed by our usual standards of customer.'

'Not for knitting. I need you to help me bolt my life back together. A road-side breakdown, you could say. Can you assist me in my hour of need?'

His words were flippant but his expression was serious. He dug deep into his pocket and retrieved something from inside.

'I'm the new girl here, so perhaps you'd rather wait for the owner to get back, although she happens to be my mother,' Steph answered, wanting to stare at him as his words sank in but hardly daring to. Was he really talking about what she thought, or was she dreaming this up?

She looked swiftly over at Emlyn the sheep as a reality check and ran a hand through her hair, hoping it looked okay.

Lately she hadn't bothered to brush it much.

Jack raised an eyebrow. He was only feet away; the counter stood between them like a referee.

'It's you I'm here for. It's my heart, you see, someone's broken it and it needs emergency rescue. You're the only one for the job.'

As he spoke Jack was thinking how much he'd missed her; how much he wanted to just jump across the counter and pull her into his arms. He'd missed so many things about her; her room-illuminating smile, her familiar smell, the way she always pulled him up sharp, her life-restoring kiss — he couldn't bear to be so near and yet so far.

Did she even realise what she did to him?

'I'm afraid we only have basic yarns and knitting patterns,' she replied, doing her usual thing of hiding behind her quirky sense of humour. 'We do have buttons and needles if you need patching up, though.' She daren't look up and meet his eyes.

'Shame,' said Jack. 'Because all I want is you. It wasn't until you walked out that I stupidly realised too late that I'd lost the one person who matters most. I've barely functioned since you left. Abercarrick doesn't matter without you and I'm not going back unless you come with me. So if you fancy a future in wool retail, then it looks like we're doing it together.'

'I'm not sure you're cut out for it. And anyway, don't you have a renewed acquaintance with your brother?'

'He's gone, back to Australia. They tried to claim they wanted to help but it was a thinly veiled way of getting their hands on a property on the estate. His business out there has hit rock bottom; seems he made rash promises and overstated himself again, but the Scottish roots return plan's off — especially as he didn't even care about seeing Dad when he was in Glen Muir. When he realised he'll never have a controlling say again, he swiftly reconsidered and high-tailed it back without much fuss.'

'Paula thinks you still love her,' Steph whispered. 'Do you?'

'I'm not sure I ever did, now that I can compare it to how I feel about you.' Jack's deep voice lowered even more, soft as velvet. 'I love you, Steph, heart and soul. I've never felt this way about anyone else.'

Steph noticed him deposit a small purple velvet box between them on the counter, drawing a small gasp from her lips and making her heart flip over.

'Fraser wants you to come back, too. We're offering you a job — just in case the offer of my love for eternity isn't quite enough to persuade you.'

Steph simply stared, her mouth forming a silent 'oh'.

'Okay, he can't offer you a London salary,' Jack pushed on. 'But it comes with accommodation. The hotel's finances are on the up now, thanks to some inspired marketing that's sending our bookings soaring.' He smiled as he pushed the little box across the counter, closer to her. 'Oh, and did I mention that I want to marry you and that's the most important part of the deal?' His eyes were bright as he looked at her hard, searching her face for response.

'Marry you?'

Jack reached forward to take her hand. 'Open the box, Steph.' He motioned at the purple trinket box.

'Jess told you, didn't she?' Steph said, starting to crumble. 'How I love you and have done since that day you bought me that umbrella and almost kissed me at Beachcomber Cove.'

'Is that so bad?' Jack asked softly. 'I've loved you ever since you created puddles in my car, told me you needed a man with muscles and turned my life on its axis.' His eyes made it plain that his words were sincere.

'Hamish and Paula have gone back to Australia,' he continued. 'Work is already underway on the stables to transform them into your brainchild business booster.' He held her hands firmly within the warmth of his fingers and went on, 'The same day Paula and Hamish left, a guy called Marios turned up demanding I give my consent for him to marry my sister. He used to work on the cruise ship and he's a builder by trade — a cracking builder as it happens, and he intends to stick around and get his teeth into the stables project. Oh, and he is going to marry Marnie, by the way.'

His gaze intensified as his fingers tightened around hers. 'So far — considering I've had a broken heart — I reckon I've done quite well against the schedule. I've taken a sabbatical from the surgery; I want to concentrate on the hotel . . . ' His eyes softened. 'And the woman I love.'

Jack pushed the little trinket box towards her and motioned for her to take it. 'You didn't think I could possibly let you just walk out of my life, did you?'

Steph repressed the urge to reach out, swallowing back the lump in her throat and the tears welling in her eyes.

'You're the best thing that's happened to me, Stephanie Baxter. I love you and I need you. Please open the box.'

With trembling fingers, she flipped it open, looking down at the ring's glimmering perfection.

'Maybe I shouldn't have worn the tux? Too much?'

At last Steph looked deep into Jack's eyes and smiled at him. He grinned as he wiped away a tear from her cheek with his thumb, then leaned forward and kissed her.

Knowing Steph the way he did, he suddenly pulled back and said, 'Oh, and Ally says we're not allowed to get married until her baby weight's all gone because she wants to wear something fitted and full of va-va-voom!'

Steph made a face. 'That's so typical of Ally!'

'Apparently she's responsible for getting us together in the first place,' he replied, punctuating his words with kisses on her neck. 'Said she had a feeling sparks would fly. She wants you to be godmother to her baby and you've to phone her as soon as the ring's on your finger.'

'Jack McGregor,' Steph said huskily, tears glittering in her eyes. 'Even Ally couldn't have anticipated what I found in you.'

Jack took out the ring and placed it where it should be. 'Now give me another kiss behind the wool shelves . . .'

Steph happily obliged — after all, there were some things even Emlyn the sheep shouldn't see.

Right now, all Steph wanted was time to adjust to having all her dreams suddenly come true — and to having Jack McGregor's ring on her finger.

THE END